IGNITE

www.chellebliss.com
CHELLE BLISS
USA TODAY BESTSELLING AUTHOR

MEN OF INKED: HEATWAVE SERIES

Book 1 - Flame

Book 2 - Burn

Book 3 - Wildfire

Book 4 - Blaze

Book 5 - Ignite

Book 6 - Spark

Book 7 - Ember

Book 8 - Singe

Book 9 - Ashes

Book 10 - Scorch

Book 11 - Torch

Book 12 - Inferno

Book 13 - Cinder

Book 14 - Dare

Inked Holiday Novella

To learn more please visit
menofinked.com/heatwave-series

IGNITE COPYRIGHT © 2020

This is a work of fiction. Names, characters, places, and incidents either are the product of the author's imagination or are used fictitiously, and any resemblance to actual persons, living or dead, business establishments, events, or locales is entirely coincidental. The publisher does not assume any responsibility for third-party websites or their content.

All Rights Reserved No part of this book may be reproduced, scanned, or distributed in any printed or electronic format without permission. Please do not participate in or encourage piracy of copyrighted materials in violation of the author's rights. Purchase only authorized editions.

Publisher © Chelle Bliss October 13th 2020
Edited by Lisa A. Hollett
Proofread by Read By Rose & Deaton Author Services
Cover Design © Chelle Bliss
Cover Photo/Model © Kevin Creekman

To my Cousin Cathy,
Thank you for keeping me sane the last four years. At least as much as any person can keep someone from losing my mind. You've been there through the hard times, good times, and when I was extra needy…which has been often.
You were my moonlight in the darkest nights.
I am forever in your debt for your love, support, and kindness.
Love Always,
Chelle

PROLOGUE

MAMMOTH

"PRINCESS."

"Don't you princess me, buddy. What the hell is going on?" There's no missing her anger in her tone, which is dripping with attitude.

I lean against the handlebars of my bike, one hand against my ear, holding the phone, and the other one hanging freely. "Club business. Can't talk about it. You know the rules."

Her breathing is heavy on the other end of the line. She's silent for a moment, but it doesn't last long before she lays into me. "Club business is always so convenient, but let me tell you something…"

"Fuck," I mutter. I raise my face toward the sky, letting the sunshine give me warmth from her icy words.

"When you call *my* family, asking them to come

help you, that makes it *my* business. So, don't you go telling me it's club business and you can't tell me anything. Pike and Jett are headed your way, and I want to know why."

"Nothing has happened. I'm near them, by myself, and my bike decided to take a shit on me. It's as simple as that."

"By yourself?" she screeches, making me wince at the shrillness in her voice. "Wait. Hold up."

So, I do that.

I wait.

I hold up, staying silent.

"Answer me," she says.

"You told me to wait," I grit out, being a smartass and already over this conversation.

"Men are impossible," she groans. "Are you seriously by yourself?" I'm pretty damn sure if she could, she'd reach through the phone and strangle me. There's no ounce of cute left in her at this moment, only anger.

"I am."

"Why would Morris and Tiny do that? You don't go anywhere alone, Mammoth. Nowhere." She draws out the last word, almost yelling it directly in my ear.

"I know that, but it was supposed to be a quick and simple job. Between my bike acting up and not being in Disciples' territory, I decided to make the call."

"You made the call, but didn't bother to call me?"

I grunt a response back without adding any words. There's nothing more to be said.

I knew what her response would be.

I knew she'd freak out and lay into me, which is what she's doing, even though I didn't make the call to her.

Fucking Gigi and Lily and their inability to keep information to themselves like all Gallo chicks. They have allegiance to one another, and nothing or no one can change that.

"I'm going to call Morris and—" she starts.

"No, Tamara. You will not. You keep your mouth shut. It's none of your business."

"Excuse me?" she whispers. "Keep my mouth shut?"

As if I don't have enough shit on my plate, a pissed-off Tamara Gallo isn't something I want added as a side dish. "Women don't get involved. I've told you that a hundred times. I don't need you calling Morris to tell him off for doing something you don't like. This is what I signed up for when I joined, Tam. I do as I'm told, and if you want me to ever get out of this life, you need to sit back, be quiet, and let me do what I have to do and do as you're told too."

"I don't like it," she grits out, probably thinking of every way she's going to torture me for laying down the law the way I just did.

"Neither do I, but I got to do what I got to do. Now, when the guys get here, I'll throw my bike in the back of the pickup, head back with them, and worry about this shit tomorrow."

"Where are you waiting?" she asks, still whispering.

I'm not fooled by the softness in her voice. I know she's pissed. I told her to keep her mouth shut, and that was a slap in the face. I could've said it nicer, explained things in a less harsh way, but Tamara never wants to listen when it comes to the club.

"A parking lot." I leave out the simple fact that it's a parking lot at a strip club. Tamara would have another fit and one I don't want to hear right now.

"Don't leave without them."

"Again, not moving until they're here, babe. I don't think my bike would make it another mile anyway. Anything else?"

"I'm mad at you," she admits like it's a revelation, but at least this time, her voice is more forceful.

"Really? I couldn't tell from all the attitude you're throwing my way."

"Don't be cute," she sasses, but I totally smile, loving when she tries to talk like me.

"You're the cute one, princess," I say, flirting with my girl.

Even if she's a pain in the ass, she's still *my* pain in the ass.

"There's no sweet-talking me, Saint," she tells me just as Gigi's pickup, with Pike and Jett inside, pulls into the parking lot.

"Gotta go. Guys are here. I'll be at your place in about an hour. I love you."

"Love you too," she mumbles. "Be careful."

"Always, princess. Always," I tell her before pressing end, happy as hell the conversation is over.

The guys are twenty feet away, waiting for a drunk guy who can barely stand upright to make his way to his car. My gaze moves from their pickup to the back of the strip club as the door swings open.

A very busty redhead in nothing more than a G-string and pasties emerges from the doorway.

But she's not alone.

There's a man behind her, pushing her to the ground as he lifts his arm. The sunshine glints off something metal in his hand, almost blinding me.

But before I have a chance to move, he fires at me.

CHAPTER
ONE

TAMARA

"MORRIS, what the fuck were you thinking?" I tap my foot, staring down at Mammoth as he lies in my bed, passed out and loaded up with painkillers.

It's been three days since Mammoth was released from the hospital after they dug the bullet out of his shoulder. I haven't talked to Morris since it happened, and I've made sure Mammoth hasn't talked to him either.

"It was supposed to be simple," Morris tells me on the other end of the phone, lucky he isn't in front of me because someone would have to pull me off him.

"Sure," I snap, unable to hold back. "Just send him across the state alone and straight into enemy territory. I may not be *in the club*, but I'm not stupid. You don't do that. I don't care if you're sending him to fuckin' Disney World for a drop, he has a brother at his side."

"Babe," Morris clips out, "I know you think you know…"

"Oh, I *do* know." I interrupt the bullshit he's about to shovel as I pace at the foot of the bed, clenching my hand into a tight fist to control the rage that's been brewing inside me for days.

I promised Mammoth I wouldn't call Morris.

I promised Mammoth I'd keep my mouth shut.

He pleaded with me to leave shit alone and that he'd handle it once he was able to, which will be when I let him out of my sight long enough to go back to the compound.

But I've had enough.

It may not be my place to speak to Morris, but I have never been good at listening or following the rules.

Badass MC or not, I'm not remaining silent and taking a back seat, no matter how many times I promise my man I will.

"We do things by ourselves all the time. What the hell do you think I run? This ain't the fuckin' Boy Scouts," he growls.

"Uh, Morris, I know you aren't the fuckin' Boy Scouts. I may not have grown up *in the life*, but I know enough that you do *not* send a brother out there alone. Not for something like he was doing."

"What was he doing?" Morris asks, putting me on the spot again.

Fucker.

He knows damn well I have no freaking clue.

Mammoth is always tight-lipped when it comes to the club and has remained so, no matter how much I bug him to confide in me.

My gaze flickers to Mammoth as I answer. "You know what he was doing."

"Refresh my memory. I'm old."

I growl, cursing under my breath. "You're not old. Stop with the bullshit. Admit your mistake and promise me it'll never happen again."

"Babe."

I stop walking, staring at the wall in front of me. "Morris."

"Come on," he says playfully.

"Say it," I demand.

He sighs. "I can't control everything."

"He. Was. Alone."

"Again, not unusual."

"He was shot, for fuck's sake."

"Happens sometimes," he mutters.

I pull the phone away from my cheek, gawking at the screen like I can somehow see his face and he can see mine. "It happens sometimes?" I whisper, filled with rage.

"Yup," he quips.

"It happens sometimes?" I whisper again, but this time slower because I can't believe his answer.

"I didn't send him to that titty bar. He was there for reasons outside of my control. So again, shit happens."

I dig my fingertips into the corners of my eyes and pinch the bridge of my nose, trying like hell to hold in my anger. "Such an asshole," I mumble, frustrated.

"Listen, kid. Is he okay?"

"He's sleeping," I say softly as I glance again at his naked body strewn across my bed with the sheet pulled up to his waist.

"So, he's alive?" he asks me again.

"You already know he is."

"If he's okay and alive, then why the hell are you busting my balls about shit that's in the past?"

"I don't want that shit to bleed into our lives, to follow him into our future. I also don't want the same shit to happen again because you send my man out there alone when he should've had a brother at his side."

"Noted," he says, and I think I finally have victory, but then he continues. "But he would still be lying in your bed with a hole in his shoulder. Maybe instead of just him being shot, one of the other guys would be too—or even worse, they'd be dead instead of still breathing like *your man.*"

I sober, thinking about Eagle, Ginger, or any of

the other guys lying on the pavement with a bullet in their head.

I wrinkle my nose, immediately feeling ill. "You know I wouldn't want that."

"Then we're on the same page."

I blink and look away from Mammoth as he starts to stir, turning my back and lowering my voice. "Not entirely."

"I listened to every word you said, but I can't control everything in the world, no matter how much you think I can."

"I know. Trust me, I know you're not God."

"Nothing to do with God, babe. I'm sorry about Mammoth. Really, I am. You know how much he means to me and the rest of the club. The last thing I wanted or expected was for him to get hurt. Enemies are coming out of the woodwork. No one will be leaving the clubhouse to go on runs or anything else without another person at their side. It's already been decided."

"Then why are you giving me such a hard time?"

He laughs. "Babe."

I stay silent and grind my teeth together.

"Listen," he says, like I'm not listening and haven't been for the last five minutes.

"I'm listening," I snarl.

"You're the one calling me, busting my chops. Placing blame where there's no blame to be placed.

Shit got fucked up, but your man is alive. Why don't you be a good woman and take care of him instead of calling me, chewing my ear off about shit I can't change?"

I open my mouth and then snap it shut as the bed creaks behind me.

"Princess," Mammoth whispers, and I freeze.

I slowly peer over my shoulder, dropping my hand to my side, trying to hide the phone, and smile. "Hey, baby."

"Who are you talking to?" Mammoth stretches, and every muscle in his body flexes underneath his ink-stained skin. He winces when he moves his arm, and the reality of the gunshot slams back into him.

"No one," I whisper, staying where I am. "Go back to sleep."

"Put the phone down," he says, patting the bed, eyes flickering between my hand and my face. "I need my woman."

"You're hurt," I tell him as Morris chirps in the background at a low rumble.

Please don't hear Morris's voice.

Please don't hear Morris's voice.

"End the call, Tamara," Mammoth demands, his eyes sliding to my leg where the phone is pressed to muffle Morris's slew of curse words. "Now."

Shit.

He heard Morris's voice.

He doesn't have to say it; I can tell by the icy look in his gray eyes.

"Grumpy," I mumble under my breath as I lift the phone and see a blank screen. I hold out my hand, showing Mammoth the screen, still digging in my heels about the phone call. "See. No one's there." Somehow, I say those words with a smile.

He shakes his head, narrowing his eyes. "I may have been shot, but I'm not deaf. I heard his voice."

"His?" I ask, tiptoeing toward my guy, trying my best to play stupid.

"I know you called Morris. I heard his voice."

Busted.

Shit.

"He just called to see how you were," I lie, still smiling like an idiot as I place my phone on the nightstand and plant my ass next to Mammoth on the bed. "I told him you were resting and that I didn't want anyone to bother you."

He reaches out with his good arm, hooking me by the waist and hauling me backward like I weigh nothing. "Princess, you're a shit liar."

"I never lie," I lie again, but I'm not backing down.

I've never been known for my ability to admit when I'm wrong. Once I dig in my heels, they're stuck, and there's no going back. It's a family trait—or maybe more of a flaw—but it's the Gallo in me.

He stares at me and doesn't even crack a smile. "Want to repeat that?"

"No," I snap.

The corner of his mouth turns up as he tightens his hand at the top of my hip. "What am I going to do with you?"

"I can think of a few things." I smirk, waggling my eyebrows. "It's a shame you're injured, though."

Always wanting to prove me wrong, he pulls me farther back until my body is flush against his. "My shoulder may be injured, but the rest of me isn't."

I turn my face up, staring into his gray eyes. "It's only been a few days, and the doctor said you need to be careful so you don't rip the staples."

He runs his fingers down the side of my arm, causing my skin to break out in goose bumps. "What does my shoulder have to do with my cock?"

"No strenuous activity, buster. Not until you're cleared by your doctor." I place my hand on his chest, toying with his piercing.

He moves his fingers from my back to my spine, making a beeline for my ass. "You know what isn't strenuous?"

"What?" I ask, squirming when his fingertips move over the swell of my ass.

"You ridin' my cock."

I giggle and slap his chest. "Stop. We're not fucking."

"Sit on my face, then."

I shake my head, biting down on my lip. God, I'd do anything to be riding his face right now instead of arguing about Morris while he has a hole in his body.

"A few more days, okay?" I beg, wanting him to have every chance to heal without any complications. "You want another pill? It'll help you sleep and get your mind off things."

"Have you ever taken one of those things?" he asks, brushing his lips against the skin of my forehead and breathing me in.

"No. Not those specifically, but something like them."

"Those pills…" He pauses and sighs. "They give me the craziest dreams."

I move out of his embrace and prop myself up, still in the crook of his arm. "What kind of dreams?"

"Sex dreams." He smirks again. "Wild sex dreams."

"Wild ones?" My eyes widen. From what I know, Mammoth's never had a tame sex life.

So, what in the world would constitute a wild sex dream?

He nods. "So, if you give me another one, you better be willing to hop on my cock because I won't be able to stop myself from finding a way to be buried deep inside you, princess."

I swallow. "No pills, then."

"No pills," he says. "Now, why don't you get that sweet ass moving and make me a sandwich?"

I blink. "Say that again, because it sounded a lot like you just ordered me to make you a sandwich."

"I'm hungry and injured, babe. If you want me to get better, I can't eat any more ramen noodles. I don't know how you eat that shit all the time. Will you please—" he emphasizes the word because my lips are twisted "—make me something with protein?"

"Since you put it that way, yes. Yes, I will. Anything to make you feel better, but just so you know —" I push myself up, staring him straight in the eyes "—in the future, make sure to throw a please in front of a statement like that or else this platinum pussy may be closed for a very long time."

He stares at me, mouth flat, studying my face. "You shittin' me?"

I shake my head, crossing my arms.

"So, do I need to say 'Can I please fuck that sweet pussy?' in the future too?" He raises a dark eyebrow.

"If you say please when we're fuckin', I'm closing the pussy shop too."

He bursts into laughter, grabbing at his shoulder when the pain slices through him, reminding him that he's injured, and he quickly sobers. "Fuck," he groans. "Don't make me laugh."

"Well, don't say dumb shit."

"Princess, you know your *pussy shop*," he says,

fighting a smile as he reaches out and strokes my leg, "will never be closed to me."

I tip my head back and laugh, fighting the tingles shooting up my thigh from his light touch. "I'm the boss of this pussy, baby. Always have been. Always will be."

His fingers inch higher, and I fight back a moan. "Is that so?"

"Yes," I say, but it doesn't come out quite as forceful or truthful as I had hoped, and I change the subject as quickly as possible. "Anyway, you're here for me to take care of you. So, let me go make you that sandwich you're so in need of, and I told Morris you won't be back until you're healed."

His eyebrows rise. "You told him that?"

"Well, maybe something like that." I shrug, hoping he'll believe me and drop it.

"What did you promise me?" Mammoth's jaw ticks.

Well, shit.

I cringe. "I know, but…"

"Tamara."

"Mammoth."

He grimaces as he adjusts his body, moving his back against the bed's headboard and his hand away from my ass. "I told you to leave shit alone."

"Well, I…he called me," I lie again.

What the hell is wrong with me?

Sometimes I can get away with bullshit, but not with Mammoth. The man can spot my lies from a mile away. Doesn't mean I'm about to change my tune. At this point, I am too entrenched in the lie to back down now. I have no other choice but to stick to my story and ride it out, even if it leads to an ass spanking, followed by a hot fuck afterward. There's always pleasure after any form of playful punishment.

Mammoth tilts his head as he rubs his shoulder, careful not to touch the bandage. Those gray eyes bore into me like he's reading my mind, knowing all the lies I've told him in the last five minutes. "Go make my sandwich," he tells me without an ounce of emotion and definitely not with any kindness.

Damn. I hate when I can't read him. "Turkey or roast beef? I think we have both."

"Both, and I'm done lying around here."

"But…" I raise a finger, ready to tell him why he's not done, no matter what he says.

He shakes his head. "No buts, Tam. I played it your way for three days. I'm well enough to get out of bed. I'm not dying, and you need to stop treating me like I am."

"Fine," I mutter, moving backward off the bed, extending my leg until my toes touch the tile floor. "I'll meet you out there, then. Want anything else?"

"My phone."

I gulp. "Sure," I say as I climb to my feet and

make my way to the dresser where I've had it turned off for the last three days. "Don't be long, okay?"

He holds out his hand, face still unreadable.

Damn.

I'm in trouble.

I know I am.

I place the cell phone in his palm and smile. "Food will be ready in five minutes."

"Close the door on your way out."

Ugh. My heart sinks. I fucked up.

Did I cross the line? Yeah. I broke the promise, but if he were in my position, he wouldn't have listened to me, no matter how many times he'd have told me he would.

I pull on a T-shirt and shorts, glancing at him from underneath my eyelashes. He watches me, phone in his hand, unmoving. I walk toward the door, ready to leave before I cry like a little bitch because he's crabby as fuck.

"Princess," he calls out before my hand touches the doorknob.

"Yeah?"

Don't turn around.

Don't do it.

Don't let him see you cry.

I'm not weak.

Not even for him.

"I'm sorry," he replies softly. "I'm not used to this."

"Me either," I whisper, turning the knob and leaving, closing the door behind me without looking in his direction.

CHAPTER
TWO

MAMMOTH

"YOU STRAIGHT?" Morris asks, not even bothering with a hello.

"As straight as an arrow. It's been hours since I've taken any meds."

I wouldn't have taken any for the pain at all, but Tamara was on my ass, losing her shit on the hour. I figured I'd let her play nurse for a few days, helping her to feel useful during a time when she felt lost and mostly afraid.

Hell, I'm not entirely fearless at this point either. I'd known I was going to live, but once again, I was faced with mortality and the possibility of death the moment the gun went off.

"Good. Now, what the fuck happened? Details are hard to come by."

I lean over the bed, arm in a sling, holding the

phone in the hand of my only functioning arm at the moment. "My bike took a shitter, so I pulled over at the Cherry Pit, figuring it was the safest place in the area. I parked around the back, staying out of sight. I called Tamara, had a short conversation with her as I waited for Pike and Jett to come and grab me and my bike. The back door opened, I saw the gun, and a second later, he shot me."

"Fuckin' hell. The Cherry Pit is supposed to be neutral."

"Well, obviously, the agreement isn't sticking. I didn't recognize the guy or see his cut, but Pike said he was a Southern Warlord."

"Fuck," Morris hisses. "Why the hell are they even in this state? This isn't their territory, and there's no fuckin' way I'm allowing them to get a foothold here."

"Since I have a hole in my body, looks like they're making their intentions known."

"Over my dead body," he replies quickly.

"You may get your wish."

He grunts. "When will you be back here?"

"Tomorrow," I tell him, knowing full well Tamara will lose her shit, but I have to be there.

I'm still a member of the club. My vote still counts; my words still have meaning. "But I can't ride. I'll probably have full movement back in a few weeks."

The last thing I want is a war with the Southern

Warlords, but I know there will be payback for what he did to me.

"We don't need you on the road with us, but I want you at the table, helping figure this shit out. There needs to be a resolution, but the last thing we need right now is an all-out war with those fuckers."

"Agreed."

"Just keep your woman busy so she isn't chewing my ear off. I have better shit to do than placate her. You got me?"

"Got the message, passed it along. But you know Tamara. I can't watch her every second of the day, but I'll do my best to keep her occupied."

"Tie her ass up or some shit. Whatever it is you do with your woman to keep her in line. I need to concentrate on other things besides having her up my ass about letting you go out alone."

"Noted, but I'm warning you now, she's probably going to drive me back there tomorrow."

"Whatever it takes to get you back here."

"Mammoth." Tamara's voice carries through the small apartment. "Come eat."

"Gotta go, brother. See you tomorrow."

"Contain her," he reminds me before disconnecting.

I try to pull on a pair of pants with one arm and fail. After thirty seconds, I yank the sling over my head, throwing it across the room. My shoulder is sore, but not anything worse than I've experienced before. I was playing by the doctor's rules to make Tamara happy, but I'm done with the pansy-ass bullshit.

After slowly putting on my jeans, I walk out of the bedroom, surprised not to see her hanging out in the hallway, keeping watch.

Tamara and Gigi are standing at the kitchen counter, huddled together whispering when I enter the room. They look at me for a moment, neither of them saying anything before they go back to whispering about whatever those two are cooking up.

They always are, too. They never leave shit alone. It's like they're genetically wired to stir up trouble.

My mouth waters the moment I see the sandwich waiting for me on the counter, a glass of water next to it, and a small bag of chips. "Thanks for the lunch, princess," I say, trying to bring my sweet back along with my patience as I slide onto the stool.

Gigi grunts, always willing to share her displeasure with me. Tamara doesn't look my way. She doesn't even acknowledge my words as she keeps her back to me, facing her cousin instead.

I grab the sandwich, take a bite, and close my eyes, letting the flavors explode across my tongue. She took the doctor's directions a little too far, feeding me soup—by which I mean ramen—and soft fruit as if I were ready for the old-age home and not healing from a small wound.

I keep my eyes on the girls, and Gigi keeps her eyes on me too, never too afraid to look away. Tamara obviously told her about what happened and how I lost my patience with her right before she left the bedroom.

It was a dick move and one I think I'll be paying for for more than a few minutes. Tamara's forgiving, but not until she's made the person feel the absolute worst. She'd make a great sadist, finding pleasure in watching a man, or a woman, writhe in pain.

I chew slowly, studying their body language. Both have their arms crossed. One facing me and the other still refusing to look in my direction. Both talking softly, barely audible to me even though I'm only a few feet away.

I drop the sandwich to the plate and lean back. "Can I have a minute with my woman?" I ask Gigi and not Tamara, because I know she'll say no, shutting me out longer than necessary.

Gigi slides her eyes to Tamara, and they exchange a look. Not a good look either, based on the way Gigi's lip curls. "I won't be far," she says, like she's warning me.

"Got it," I tell her, not moving a muscle.

She starts to walk away but moves slower than a snowbird stumbling through a parking lot.

Once I hear her bedroom door close, I move my gaze to Tamara. Actually, to her back because she hasn't bothered to face me yet. "Princess, look at me."

"No," she says softly, looking straight ahead to the cupboards on the opposite wall.

"I fucked up," I admit. "I'm sorry."

"You did fuck up." Her shoulder drops, but she still doesn't turn toward me. "You made me feel like shit when all I'm trying to do is help you."

I push away from my sandwich and make my way around the counter to stand in front of her. Raising my hand, I touch her face, and she doesn't move away. "Listen, love," I plead, swiping my thumb across her cheek, feeling the dampness against my skin. "I didn't mean to be a dick. The pills make me loopy and crabby as hell too. I hate feeling like a burden and having you wait on me like I'm an invalid. I'm the one who's supposed to be taking care of you, not the other way around."

She keeps her hazel eyes down, not giving me the thing I want the most. "You're not a burden. If it were me who was injured, would you think of me like that?"

"Of course not. I'd do everything in my power to make you better. I love you too much to watch you suffer and not do something."

She tips her face back, staring up at me, tears resting near her eyelashes, ready to fall. "Goddamn you. I'm not a crier. I've never been a crier, but you were such an asshole, Mammoth. You never treat me that way. Never. It just threw me, hearing you order me to make you a sandwich. I thought we'd gone backward about fifty years in time and I should find a set of pearls to put around my neck so I could become Little Suzy Homemaker."

I cringe at her words. "Listen, I didn't mean it that way. My head's foggy, and I don't feel like myself. I should've said please and asked if you could make me something to eat. I'm sorry, princess. Truly sorry."

"You should be," she whispers, moving her face into my palm, melting into my touch.

"Why the tears, Tam? I know there's more to this than a sandwich. I mean, the woman I know would've told me to just shove the sandwich right up my ass, given me the middle finger, and slammed the door as she marched her fine ass out."

She leans forward, falling into my chest, smashing her face against my skin. "I don't think I've ever been so scared," she whispers and wraps her arms around my body, holding me so damn tight I'm almost winded.

But I don't dare move.

I don't speak.

Hell, I'm barely breathing.

Although I was pissed when the argument started about something unimportant, this conversation is about something else…something that's changed her. She needs to get this off her chest, and I'm not about to stop her by opening my mouth. I'm going to give her what she needs and hold her as tightly as possible, letting her get everything out.

"When Pike called, I thought you were going to die," she confesses. "I lost my mind. Images of you lying on the gravel at some shithole, bleeding out…" She shakes her head, rubbing her tears into my skin. "I didn't think I'd ever get to see your face again. Touch your skin. Feel the warmth of your arms around me, holding me, comforting me."

"Baby, I'm fine. Pike shouldn't have—"

"No," she interrupts, tipping her head back and gazing up at me with her eyes blazing. "He told me everything. He didn't freak out. He didn't say you were dying. But my mind went there. I allowed myself to feel that fear. I know the longer you're across the state, living with the Disciples, the closer we come to the day when I really get the phone call that you were shot and didn't make it. What if next time it isn't a shoulder wound? We were lucky. The guy had shit aim, but what if he'd moved the gun just a few more inches? He could've shot you right in the chest, stopping this heart." She places her hand in the middle of my chest, right over my heart. "What would I have done then?"

I bend my neck, placing my lips against her forehead. "It won't happen."

"It could," she tells me.

"It won't. I won't be in the club long enough or put myself in a situation like that again. I'll talk to Tiny and Morris. We'll speed up my exit. They'll understand. This wound—" I dip my chin toward the bandage on my shoulder "—will get me what we want earlier than we expected."

"They already said you'll never be free."

I pull her closer, resting my cheek against her soft hair as she snuggles into my chest. "No one leaves completely, but I'll be as free as anyone can be. I won't have to be a part of them day-to-day. I won't have to wear my cut, making myself a target. I won't have to go on spur-of-the-moment rides. Sure, I may be called upon if shit goes sideways or if they need a favor over here, but other than that, I'll be more out than in."

She sighs, running her hand down my back, tracing the line of my spine. "I need you to be here more than you're there."

"Done."

"I need you in my bed at night."

"I'll make it happen."

"I need to grow old with you."

"I'd have it no other way," I promise her, meaning every fucking word.

She stares up at me with so much hope. "I want babies with you. Lots of babies."

I swallow, trying to push down the fear I've always had about being a shit father. "Whatever you want, princess. You know I'd give you the moon and the stars if I could reach high enough."

"At least you have time to recuperate before you have to go back to the compound."

I stiffen, and her eyes widen.

"Do not tell me you're going back already."

"I have to go back tomorrow. They need me there, and I don't have a choice. I'm still a member of the club, injured or not."

She sighs, dropping her head to the middle of my chest again. "Fuckers," she murmurs against my skin, digging her fingernails into my back. "You can't ride like this."

"I'll have Pike drive me," I tell her, hating that I have to ask anyone to drive me across the entire state and can't do it myself.

"No," she says quickly, keeping her face pressed into me. "I'll take you."

"I don't think—"

"I don't care. I'll take you. You need a ride. I'm your ride. This isn't up for discussion or debate. Understand?"

A smile spreads across my face because I do like it

when she's bossy…at least, sometimes I do. Other times, not so much. "You can take me, then."

She peers up, a smirk finally back on those beautiful lips. "I wasn't asking for your permission."

"We good, then?"

She nods. "Always."

"I'm yours today. What do you want to do?"

"I want you to finish eating and then go back to bed."

I sigh.

"But I'm going to be in that bed with you, baby. We'll see if you can handle me before I bring you back to the compound. We'll call it a test."

I smile, liking her way of thinking. "You going to grade me?" I lift an eyebrow.

She laughs. "Of course."

I slide my hand down to her ass. "Will there be extra credit?"

She moves her hand into the waistband of my jeans. "It's possible, but it won't be easy."

"I'm up for the challenge, princess."

"I'm sure you are," she says, winking.

CHAPTER
THREE

TAMARA

I GASP, sucking in air like I've had my head underwater for more seconds than humanly possible. "Jesus fucking Christ," I mutter, collapsing back against the mattress.

"Princess, Jesus had nothing to do with that."

I close my eyes, my head spinning from lack of oxygen and the orgasmic aftershocks that are still coursing through my body. "I'm pretty damn sure I saw God."

"He didn't have anything to do with it either," he says, smiling down at me with total and complete adoration. "That was all me, baby."

I wave my hand at him before quickly dropping it to the bed, too tired from the two orgasms he so willingly and selflessly gave me.

"Well, we know your mouth is in working order."

"Fingers too," he adds, wiggling those long, thick bad boys in the air as he stands, dick at attention, waving around, letting himself be known. "But I think my cock needs a check."

I laugh, unable to take my eyes off his beautiful fuckstick. "Well, get on up here and show me what you got," I tell him.

He shakes his head. "Bum shoulder, remember? Get your ass down here," he tells me, standing at the end of the bed, waiting. "On all fours, ass in the air. You know how I like it."

My belly flutters, and somehow, my pussy twitches. The greedy bitch actually wants more, but the rest of me is waving the white flag, begging for a break. "I don't know if I can hold myself up after all that."

"Sweetheart," he says softly, smirking, "just place that beautiful face against the mattress, and I'll do the rest. I won't let you fall."

I move like my ass is on fire, scrambling to the end of the bed. I assume the position, ass up, my face smashed against the rumpled sheets, arms at my sides, and wait, panting like a cat in heat.

"Perfect," he whispers, running his hand down the side of my hip. "Just perfect."

We hadn't seen each other in two weeks before he landed in the hospital, a hole blown into his body. Usually when we saw each other again, we did nothing else except fuck, sleep, and eat. I looked forward to these days. The countless orgasms followed by the naps in his arms afterward.

I sneak a peek, staring down the side of my legs, watching him as he admires my ass. There's always a hunger in his eyes. Always a thirst he never seems to quench, no matter how many tastes or sips he has of me. "You going to stare at it all day, or are you going to fuck me?" I say, feeling sassy.

Before I can even smile, he lifts his hand, bringing it down fast and not all that hard against my ass. It's just enough pain to send a jolt through my system and cause me to push my ass up higher.

He runs his palm over the very spot that still stings, soothing me. "You want to say that again?"

"Kind of." I laugh, wiggling my butt around. "But I'd prefer if you'd put your cock inside me instead of playing games."

"This cock, princess?" he asks, removing his hand from my ass and wrapping it around his long, thick shaft. "You want this one?"

I lick my lips, almost salivating at the sight. "Yes," I murmur, unable to stop staring as he strokes himself.

"Beg for it," the fucker tells me, smirk firmly planted on his face, his gray eyes staring right into mine.

I stop shaking my ass. "Beg?"

"Tell me how much you want this cock."

I lift up on my elbows and give him a smirk right back. "Baby," I whisper, sweeping my gaze up his body, away from his cock, to his face. "You've already given me two amazing orgasms. I'm pretty damn good right now. I think you should be the one begging for the orgasm at this point. But if you don't want it and would rather stroke that fine cock yourself, I'll be more than happy to watch."

"Fuckin' impossibly cute," he mutters, still moving his hand up and down, up and down, in a slow and steady rhythm.

"Why don't you beg for my luscious pussy?" I say to him, holding in my laughter because I know I'm going to pay for this, and I sound completely ridiculous. "Beg for the chance to stick that aching cock into my tight, wet pussy."

He sucks in a breath, and I know he's about to lose it.

I'm getting to him.

I'm toying with him in much the same way he toys with me.

There's power in it, and it's addictive.

"Beg, Mammoth. Tell me how badly you want my cunt."

His eyes flash with hunger. The word "cunt" pushed him over, bringing out the animal part of him. The side of him that's filled with lust and the need to spill his seed. He takes a step forward, moving toward me with his dick ready for action.

When the tip of his penis touches my body, I inch forward and get a growl as a response.

"Beg," I remind him.

"I don't beg."

I raise an eyebrow, still propped up, waiting. "You don't, but you will."

He smiles down at me, and I think I've won. My inner cheerleader is already doing spirit fingers, celebrating our victory and the pounding I'm about to receive for my good deeds.

But to my surprise, he doesn't beg.

He doesn't open his mouth.

Instead, he sits down next to me, shoulder touching my hip, and continues to move his hands up and down his shaft.

"What are you doing?" I ask, blinking and gawking at him in all his sexy glory.

"I don't beg, and you're right, my hand works too."

"Asshole," I growl under my breath.

He closes his eyes and continues working his cock in his palm, slowing down near the tip before moving his closed fist lower, repeatedly.

I don't wait around too long because I've been waiting for this moment since the last time he said goodbye. I crawl backward until my feet touch the floor and stand in front of him.

"Are you really going to jack off?" I ask him, mesmerized and unable to stop staring. If I weren't so hungry for his cock, I'd stay like this, watching him pleasure himself. But fuck, I'm not. I'm needy and greedy. Self-restraint has never been my strong suit, especially when it comes to Mammoth.

"Mmm," he mumbles, stroking faster, squeezing harder.

I push his hand away and straddle his legs, hovering above his length. "You're a fucker, baby," I whisper, running my finger down the side of his face, staring into his gray eyes. "But let me remind you how much better my pussy is compared to your hand."

He reaches out, placing his hand on my hip. "Teach me a lesson," he teases, his eyes dipping to my tits. "Give me some sweet punishment."

I snake my arm around his good shoulder, resting my hand at the back of his neck, careful not to touch anywhere near his bandages. "Hold on, because I'm about to rock your world."

He digs his fingertips into my hip and growls, telling me he likes my dirty talk even though it's lame as hell.

I bend my head forward, taking his lips with mine as I lower my bottom and grab his cock with my free hand, lining up our bodies.

He moans his approval as I push myself down, enveloping just the tip.

"You like this?" I ask, whispering against his lips, feeling his body tense underneath me.

"Yes," he whispers back, opening his eyes to stare at me. "I've missed this. I've missed you. I need that sweet cunt, princess. I *need* you."

Did he beg? Not really.

But did he say all the magical words? Yes.

I am done playing games.

Done trying to one-up each other.

I need Mammoth too.

I need his cock.

I need the connection.

I've already had two orgasms, and I'll always take more, but I want to feel connected with him in the most biblical way.

My fingers tighten around the back of his neck as his dig into my hip, both of us tethered to each other before I drop down, impaling myself on his length.

His mouth opens, tongue sweeping inside mine, as we both moan in pleasure. His chest is rock hard when I smash my tits against him, loving the warmth of his body and the softness of his skin. I raise myself up and slam my lower half down, over and over again until he's kissing me so hard, I know my lips are going to be sore and swollen.

He slides his hand to my ass, grabbing me

roughly as I ride him, moving quicker with each passing stroke. My greedy pussy convulses as the third orgasm of the day crashes over me, milking his cock, wanting to give him the same pleasure. I haven't even made it over the first wave of pleasure when he tightens his grip on my ass, following me off the cliff.

We sit there for a moment, me in his lap, his hand still on my ass, both of us gasping for air.

"I love you," he whispers.

I rest my forehead against his, gazing into his hauntingly beautiful eyes. "I love you too," I say back, pushing away the feelings of fear I had a few days ago when I thought I could lose him forever.

Mammoth collapses backward, taking me with him, and I roll to his good side, nuzzling into him. His fingers glide up my back, burrowing in my hair. "What's the one thing you want that you don't have now?" he asks, staring up at the ceiling.

I close my eyes, exhaustion after three orgasms slowly taking over. "I have what I want," I tell him, referring to us. "I'm content."

"I don't want you to be content. You deserve more than contentment. You deserve everything you want and more."

"I'm good. Really good." I snuggle into him harder, resting my cheek against his chest. "Life is about to get better too. I'll be done with school soon, and you'll be here with me full time and out of the club. What more is there?"

"There's so much more, princess."

I tip my head back, looking up at him. "What do you want?"

"I want a house where we can have privacy. I want my own business so I can be my own boss. I want babies, lots of babies, running around with their wild hair blowing in the wind and their infectious smiles making every day brighter."

"Slow your roll, tootsie pop."

He laughs, brushing his lips against my forehead. "Five kids. Think about how great that would be."

My vagina literally aches thinking about squeezing five babies out of my body. He's clearly still high on the pain meds because there's no way I'm having five kids.

I blink, furrowing my brows. "Two."

"Four."

"Three."

"Perfect," he says and smirks.

Damn.

I walked right into that one.

"I hated being an only child," he confides in me. "I don't want that shit for my kid."

"Funny because I always wished I was an only child."

"We don't have to have them right away," he tells me.

Well, thank God for that.

"What are you going to do after college? Have you started thinking about where you're going to work? We need to make a plan."

I chew the inside of my lip, realizing I haven't spent much time thinking about the future. At least not beyond graduation and Mammoth. "I don't know. I've never been much of a planner."

"We got to get our shit together. Time's passing, and we're standing still. We could work together. Be a team."

I raise up on one arm, staring down at him as he lies against my purple comforter. "You want to work together?"

He smiles. "Why not?"

"We'd be at each other's throats."

"Make-up sex and hate-fucking are the best," he tells me, keeping a straight face while saying those words.

I think about it.

There's some truth to what he's saying.

Sure, hate-fucking has its bonuses.

The intensity is always high and the emotions more intense, but that doesn't mean I want to be around him twenty-four hours a day, seven days a week.

I love him more than anyone in the world, but I also like a little alone time.

"Come on. Why work for someone else when we can build something together? I'm buying Tank's garage from him. We already worked out all the details. Don't you want to work with me?" He pouts, laying it on so damn thick.

"What the hell would you have me do? I can't fix things. My math skills are absolute shit unless you're asking me the discounted price for an item on a sale rack. What use could I possibly be to you?"

"I don't want a small-town garage. I'm not looking to spend my days replacing tires and brakes. I want this thing to be big. I want to be known as the best of the best for custom restorations of vintage cars. Your degree is in marketing, yeah?"

"It will be."

"I need a marketer. I need someone to blow up my social media and get the garage noticed. Why would I hire someone else when my woman can do the best job? We could build the life we want without having to worry about anyone else or answering to someone who doesn't give a shit about us."

"I don't know." I run my finger across his chest, pausing near his nipple piercing. "I'm not sure it's a good idea. I love you, but I don't know if the around-the-clock thing is the greatest idea you've ever had."

"Listen, we'll set up an office for you, but you can work at home if you'd prefer. You don't need to be in the shop with me and the other guys. Just promise me you'll think about it, princess. It's going to be fuckin' fantastic."

"Have you seen the garage?" I wrinkle my nose. "It's old and a complete mess."

"It's cheap and has everything we need. It'll take a little work, but I can have that baby humming and looking like new in no time, especially by the time you graduate."

He's right.

The building is solid but needs some repairs. Tank hasn't done much in the last few years to make the place look pretty. He always says it's meant to look dirty because it's a garage and not a bland, generic corporate location. He's all about the work and not the aesthetics of the joint. Which is more than clear to anyone driving by the dingy place.

"You really want to do this together?" I ask, letting those words sink in.

"This is all about us and our three little boys."

"Three little girls," I correct him, poking him in the chest.

"Two boys and a girl," he shoots back.

"Whatever."

"But that poor girl. She'll be all alone. She'd love a sister."

"Stop." I roll my eyes. "We're not having four kids."

"We'll see," he mutters, closing his eyes.

"No. No. No."

"Mmm," he mumbles. "So, will you take the job?"

Jesus.

He's making my head spin.

He's popping back and forth between too many topics.

He's wearing me down.

Something he likes to do when he wants things I'm not necessarily one hundred percent on board with.

"We'll see. We have plenty of time."

"Just think about it."

"I will."

"I'm serious," he says.

"Me too. I said I'll think about it."

"Good," he whispers. "Six babies."

I chew my lips and think about everything he said. About the garage. About working together. About our babies. About Mammoth in my life forever, and everything we could build together.

And as I fall asleep, I dream of our future.

CHAPTER
FOUR

MAMMOTH

THE DRIVE to the compound is long and abnormally quiet. Tamara usually talks my ear off the entire way when she's with me, but today, she's silent. I've tried to talk to her a few times, but every response has been clipped and usually given to the window instead of turning to face me with her reply.

I understand why, but it doesn't make the time pass any faster or keep the silence from being overwhelmingly deafening.

She is stewing over the fact that I could've died, even though I didn't. The thought of losing me has been chewing at her insides for days now, planting a firm hold in her head, allowing the seeds of fear to sprout roots.

When we finally make it to the clubhouse, she

marches straight to the bar and plops down on a stool, giving every person inside the stink eye.

None of the guys will say shit to her because she's mine. I think they are afraid of her too, but they'll never admit it. They also know the happy, playful, and troublemaking Tamara far better than the one whose anger is currently festering as she sits at the bar, tapping her fingernails against the wood.

"Keep your fine ass there," I tell her, pointing to the spot.

I want to make sure we're both clear on where she should be and stay. The last thing I need is her stirring up anything while I am busy with Tiny and Morris.

Every time she comes here, she starts trouble, especially with the women, and I don't have the time or the patience to clean up her mess today.

I know the jealous bitches target her, hating that she's with me and somehow feeling slighted. I never would've been with them anyway, but they never seemed to believe me when I said as much.

Tamara lifts up her hands, leaning back in the stool. "Where else would I go?" she says, giving me lip and tons of attitude.

I tilt my head, staring at her. "I'm serious."

She smiles devilishly. "Me too."

"I got her, brother. I'll watch her," Eagle says to me, resting an arm against the bar, sipping a beer. "Her ass won't move."

"Technically," she says, raising a finger, "my ass will move, but not off this stool."

I grunt and shake my head.

The woman is impossible and difficult, but goddamn, I'm nuts about her. Maybe I am the crazy one, keeping her around even when she makes my life challenging.

But in the balance of sanity and crazy, the good outweighs the bad, and she brings so much love into my life when I never thought I'd find it.

"Mammoth!" Morris's voice booms through the room, making everyone jump except me. "Get your ass in here and stop fuckin' around with your woman."

"You heard the man." Tamara shoos me away. "We'll just be here, catching up and talking about you."

Eagle's eyes slide to mine, and he shrugs. "Just go," he tells me with a chin lift. "I got this. I'll handle her."

Tamara raises an eyebrow, a crooked smile on her face. She loves when men try to "handle her." She and Eagle have spent enough time together; they get each other. He's the one guy I know, besides me, who will put up with her shit and keep on rolling.

"Fucking hell," I mutter, moving toward Morris as he stands in the doorway, arms crossed, mean mug firmly planted on his face.

I have attitude coming from all sides, and I'm the one with a hole in my body.

Morris's gaze bounces between my face and my shoulder, taking two passes before he turns his back, walking into the room. "Close the door," he says before my boots make it fully inside the space.

Tiny's at the opposite end of the room, sitting at the table, flipping the lid of his Zippo lighter open and closed, over and over again. "Sit," he tells me, eyes dipping to the open seat. "It's time to talk."

It's almost like I'm the one who's about to be grilled over something I did wrong, when I'm the one who got shot for breaking down in the wrong place at the wrong time.

I sit, staring down the long table, remaining silent until Morris takes a seat next to Tiny like he always does. "I'm ready to talk," I say when all three of us are seated. "Let's get this over with."

Tiny places his lighter on top of a pack of cigarettes before leaning forward, clasping his hands. "The man who shot you is being dealt with," Tiny announces.

"He went rogue from his club and was acting against the wishes of his Prez." There's a smile behind Morris's palm as he moves his hand across his face. "The hit on you was not sanctioned, but the retaliation for his offense was, and the matter is now closed."

Just like that…it's done. I got no say in anything even though I'm the one who took the bullet.

My leg begins to move, up and down, up and down, underneath the table, releasing the energy and rage I feel toward Morris and Tiny for not including me in the conversation.

"But we'll talk more about it tomorrow," Morris adds, staring down the table at me.

"As for your time with the club," Tiny continues, staring down the length of the table as he crosses one arm over his chest and places the opposite hand on his beard. "What did the doctors say about your shoulder?"

"They said it'll heal, and I'll probably need therapy for a few months to get back full use of the muscles that were damaged."

Tiny turns to Morris, exchanging a look before he speaks. "We know you want out. We know you've been chomping at the bit since you fell for that woman and had a taste of her sweetness."

"I do," I tell them, having stated all this before. "I know there will be strings, but I want to be as close to her as possible and start whatever life I can with her at my side. You know she's not built for this life. She wouldn't be a good fit."

"You can say that again," Morris mutters. "Since you're of no use to us here if you can't ride, we feel it's time for you to start opening up shop on the other coast and get yourself set up."

"Okay," I say, trying to keep the happiness out of my voice. I figured I still had a good eight months left before they'd give me permission to leave, but maybe the shooting was a blessing in disguise.

"You're still a Disciple. Still a brother. We're giving you more leeway than we've given others in the past," Tiny adds.

"I know." I nod, fully understanding the opportunity they're giving me by allowing me to leave and keep breathing. "I'm thankful for that."

"You've always done what's best for the club. You are not only a brother by name, but by oath and action," Morris adds.

"This is my family too," I remind them, remembering how lost I felt after I left the military and somehow found myself prospecting for the MC.

I've always prided myself on my loyalty and being a man of my word. If it weren't for Tamara, I'd probably have spent my life within the MC, eventually landing an old lady and raising my kids around a group of men who'd always have my back.

"This is not a free pass. You understand what I'm saying?" Tiny studies my face.

I nod.

"If we need you, when we call, you'll do what's

asked. Your freedom only extends as far as we'll allow it to reach."

"Got it." I lean back in the chair, stretching my legs. "Once a Disciple, always a Disciple."

"I hate to see you go," Tiny says, breaking with his usual tough-as-nails bullshit. "I understand why you're going but doesn't mean I'm happy about it."

"I know," I tell him, trying not to get sentimental.

I had so many good times here.

Hell, great times, even. But there's a time when every man must move on, and my time is now.

"I found something too good to let slip through my fingers."

Tiny sighs. "Figured it would happen sooner or later. I was just hoping it was with one of *our* girls."

Morris shakes his head. "He needed someone who was going to challenge him, and the women around here are not that," Morris adds. "His girl, the one sitting out there giving shit to Eagle, she was made for him. Can't deny the connection. I saw it the moment they met. I knew then as much as I do now, she would take him away."

Tiny grunts. "Stay the night to celebrate with us, yeah?"

"Of course," I tell them, not feeling like getting back in the car with Tamara for a silent ride home. "I wasn't planning on packing until tomorrow."

A shadow passes across Morris's face as he inhales, letting the reality settle over him.

I am really leaving, and there isn't anything that will change that.

I go to stand, but Tiny motions for me stay put, and I place my ass back in the seat, knowing we aren't done.

"One more thing," Tiny says, placing his arms on the table, flattening his palms against the wood. "We want to talk to you about the garage."

"The garage stays legit," I tell him, pointing a finger at him. "It's going to be Tamara's business as well as mine, and I can't have the MC interfering or fucking that up."

Tiny scrubs a hand down his face, cursing into his palm. "We'll find another way to do what we need to do."

"Want to clue me in?"

Tiny shakes his head. "Not yet. Once we have more information, we'll fill you in. You're now on a need-to-know basis."

I don't say another word. I'm surprisingly okay with it. I'm more than okay. I feel at peace, not having to worry about their next scheme to make money and trying to figure out how to run the operation while staying under the radar of the Feds.

"I want this shit thought out. I'm not leaving here,

going to the other coast, just to have my ass land in jail for something stupid."

"It'll be worth it," Morris tells me, eyes pinned on mine.

"No amount of money is worth a stint in prison, Morris. None."

"Everyone has a price," Tiny adds, resting his tattooed hand over his mouth. "Even you."

I shake my head. "I got a good thing going and an even better future planned. Whatever you two are cooking up better be solid and low risk. I'm not going down for stupid shit. I have enough money saved to last me more than a few years, and with the shop opening and eventually that income rolling in, I don't need whatever you're going to offer."

"Never say never." Morris smiles. "Your woman likes to live a certain way. She also likes pretty things. Can't keep her in that life if you're piss-poor broke, struggling to launch a business."

I laugh. "Tamara has her own money. She doesn't *need* me to buy her expensive things. She's the first woman I've ever been with who doesn't want anything other than my time."

"Fuckin' Gallos," Morris mutters, shaking his head.

"Now, are we done?" I raise an eyebrow, staring at the two men I spent too many nights raising hell with over the last handful of years.

"We're done," Tiny announces, pushing back from the table and rising to his feet. "For now."

I nod, standing too. "I'll be gone tomorrow."

Morris stalks toward me, stopping a foot away, and places his hand on my shoulder. "There's no need to rush. We're not clocking you or keeping track of your time. Leave when you want to leave. Stay if you want to stay. Just know you're always welcome, always a Disciple."

We have an uncomfortable moment where Morris stares at me, swallowing down something he wants to say but doesn't, before his hand drops down and he walks away without another word.

"Shit's changing. Always changing," Tiny mumbles before walking out right behind Morris.

I stand there for a moment, staring around the room I've spent countless hours in over the years.

Time spent planning things I never thought I'd get involved with but somehow did.

Time spent planning a future that never came to fruition.

Time wasted, but somehow not.

Without all the moments between these walls, I never would've met the spitfire waiting for me outside the door, no doubt still giving Eagle shit and loving every second of it too.

Without my time here, I never would've had a future.

I BLINK, staring at Mammoth, not believing the words coming out of his sexy mouth. "Say it again," I say softly, scared if I talk any louder, his response will change.

"I've been given the go-ahead to move. We can finally start our life together."

My mouth opens and closes as I process what he's telling me, but I'm not able to believe it. "Why now?"

He smiles, brushing his fingers against my face. "Bum shoulder and my inability to ride aren't really qualities an MC looks for in a brother."

"Really?" I gawk at him, still not believing what he's telling me. "This isn't anything to joke about, Mammoth."

If he's pulling my leg, I'll be so pissed. He wouldn't do that to me, though, would he?

"Look at my face, princess. Does it look like I'm joking?"

I study his face as he stands in front of me, touching my cheek. All I see is joy and relief etched across his beautiful features. "You're not shitting me?"

"No." He laughs, smiling down at me. "I'm not shitting you."

I leap up, throwing my arms around his shoulders and peppering his cheeks with kisses. "This is the best news ever, baby." I squeeze him so damn tight.

"Tam," he says, his voice strained. "Shoulder."

I move back, wincing. "I forgot," I tell him, retracting my hands. "I'm sorry."

"I can take a little pain for you, princess."

I feel as if I'm floating on air. What a whirlwind of emotions. A few days ago, he was lying in the hospital, a hole blown in his shoulder, and now he finally has his walking papers from the Disciples.

Maybe the shooting was a blessing in disguise. If something as awful as that ever can be. But in reality, without his injury, he would've been required to be here at least another eight months.

"Totally the best news ever." I smile, unable to keep the smile from my face. "You can stay in my room at the apartment while I'm away at school during the week, until we find a place. I'll come home every weekend."

Mammoth shakes his head. "Gigi and I wouldn't make the best roommates."

I furrow my brows. "Why?"

"With you away, I wouldn't feel right staying in her place alone with her. Understand?"

I nod. I do understand. I mean, I get the logic, but it doesn't make it wise or reality. If I could trust anyone in the world with Mammoth, it would be her.

"She's never there. If you stay at our place, she'll stay at Pike's. End of story," I tell him, putting my proverbial foot down.

He stares at me, jaw ticking, gray eyes searching mine. "It's still a no."

"Just for a few days until you find a place."

"*Our* place," he corrects me. He smiles, pulling me closer with one arm hooked around my body, hand on my ass. "I just need a bed. We can save finding a place for later."

I dig my fingers into his hair, careful not to touch his shoulder.

"I could live in the apartment above the office at the garage."

I chew on my lip, letting him work through that statement.

"It's small, but more than enough," he says, not backing off that idea.

"Um," I mumble, trying to keep my face as

emotionless as possible, but also knowing I'm failing miserably.

"It's perfect."

"Mammoth," I whisper, hating to break the news to him that I am not built for the garage lifestyle.

"Princess," he says, smiling down at me as I stand between his legs, toying with his long brown hair.

"I can't live in a garage," I tell him, ignoring the knot forming in my stomach.

He laughs, giving my thigh a squeeze. "It won't be forever. When you graduate, we'll find our own place. It's the perfect go-between for now. I'll be at the garage all the time working anyway. There's no point in wasting money on a rental when you're not going to be around to enjoy it with me."

"So, what you're saying is I better get used to the smell of motor oil and gasoline?"

"I'll burn those fancy chick candles you love so much. You can make the place smell like pumpkin whatever-the-fuck-it's-called."

"Pumpkin spice," I correct him.

He nods, smiling back at me.

"You love me," I whisper.

He nods again, brushing my hair away from my face. "Was there any doubt?"

"The pumpkin spice sealed the deal. Before that, I wasn't entirely convinced. But any man who agrees to burn pumpkin spice to make his woman happy has to be in love. What else could it be?"

"You're out of your mind."

I laugh. "Was there any doubt?"

He bends his neck, bringing his mouth to mine. The kiss is soft and gentle, making my toes curl. "I want you back in school tomorrow," he whispers against my lips.

I open my eyes, staring at him with our faces close together. "Tomorrow? I have to take care of you, and who's going to drive you back to the other coast?"

Mammoth slides his hand up my spine, cupping the back of my head. "My truck is here. I can drive myself, and you've already missed enough school. It's a shoulder, Tamara. I can survive with one arm."

I pull my head back, wanting to see his entire face. "It's not a good idea. It's too dangerous."

"Driving with one arm is dangerous?"

I nod, keeping my face straight and serious. "Extremely dangerous."

"Not any more dangerous than being in a car with you when you're using two hands."

"I'm a great driver," I scoff.

"Your bumper and fender would say otherwise."

"There're a lot of blind spots when I'm parking. It's not my fault."

He raises an eyebrow, knowing I'm full of shit.

I am a horrible driver, but I don't drive any worse

or better than most everybody in the state of Florida. It's the reason I haven't had a new car in years. There's no point with the miles I put on driving back and forth between college and home. Once I graduate and don't have to do the I-75 driver dash every few days, I'll be able to keep a car in pristine condition.

Mammoth tightens his grip around the back of my neck, pulling my face closer again. "School tomorrow. Understand?"

I twist my lips and mutter, "Fine." Which is the exact opposite of how I feel about abandoning him during his time of need.

"School is too important, and you're too close to finishing to fuck it all up for me. I've been taking care of myself for a long time, babe. I can do it for a few days right now with one arm, and if I need anything, Pike, Gigi, Lily, Jett, and probably anyone from your family will be there to help."

"Promise me you'll stay in my room for a few days at least until you and Tank work out the details. Don't go trying to move in to that dirty-ass garage while you have an open wound that's trying to heal."

He sighs, but I raise an eyebrow back at him because he has to know my logic isn't wrong. If he wants me to give a little and go back to school, he needs to give a little too and at least try to stay healthy.

"Fine," he bites out, just as annoyed at being told what to do as I am.

"Then we're agreed."

"I'll spend at least the first week in your apartment until I'm more healed, and your sweet ass is heading back to school."

I smile. "It's a deal. I'll even tell Gigi not to fawn over you too much while I'm gone, but make no mistake, I will be calling her to make sure you're not overdoing things."

Mammoth pushes me back until I'm flush against the bed and he's on top of me, propped up on his uninjured arm. "Absolutely no fawning."

I swallow, staring up into his seemingly bottomless gray eyes. "No fawning," I repeat, whisper-soft.

"I'm a grown man."

I nod as I slide my hands across his back, feeling every ridge and dip until they meet in the middle over his spine. "You're grown."

"I don't have anyone parked outside your apartment on campus to make sure you're not doing anything crazy."

"I never do anything crazy."

He stares at me, waiting for me to crack and knowing damn well I do stupid shit all the time.

"Well, not always," I finally admit. "My course load is too heavy this year for shenanigans anyway."

"Thank fuck for small miracles," he says against

my lips as he steals my breath along with another piece of my heart.

How have I fallen so fast and so hard for this man?

He's everything I said I wouldn't love but somehow can't resist.

It's like God wanted to play the greatest cosmic joke on me and remind me that I'm not the kick-ass independent chick I always thought I was.

I used to think my mother was crazy as hell for putting up with my father, but now I get it. I understand her ability to look past his faults, of which there are many, and to focus only on his good.

Mammoth isn't an easy man, nor is he a perfect man. But he is perfect for me and easier than most. I've had my fair share of bad relationships. "Toxic Tamara" could've been my nickname before, but the day I met Mammoth, everything changed.

I have a man who loves me. One who cares about me, my well-being, and my pleasure. I've hit the hottie badass biker jackpot without becoming an old lady. Thank God. I would've done a shit job at staying in the background, seen and not heard—no Gallo girl is ever good at staying silent.

Mammoth lifts himself up with his one good arm and stares down at me. "There're still a few hours of sunshine left. I want you back on campus before sundown and ready for class in the morning."

My frown is immediate and severe. "I'll leave in the morning."

He shakes his head. "I want you to get a good night's rest and get your shit in order. I don't want you fighting rush-hour traffic, frantic that you're late, and tired as hell from a night here at the compound." He pushes up, kneeling between my legs.

I gape up at him, my mouth opening and closing, ready to argue.

"And before you give me any lip, you know I'm right," he says before I have a chance to speak.

I narrow my eyes, hating that he is, because I want nothing more than to lie in this bed, curled up in his arms all night. "Tomorrow's Thursday. Maybe I should just skip it and start fresh on Monday."

"You've already missed enough school, Tamara. We're not going to have an argument about this."

I pout, crossing my arms over my chest as I stare up at him. "I'm not ready to go."

His facial features soften. "I'm fine. I'll continue to be fine too. I'm breathing and don't need you falling further behind just so you can stare at me. Get your ass up, and get on the road."

I sit up and flatten my palms against the mattress, tilting my head. "Is that an order?"

Mammoth laughs, shaking his head, knowing I'm being difficult and already used to my bullshit. "It's an order, princess."

"One last fuck?" I ask, hoping to buy myself a little bit of time with my pussy.

"You can have some more dick in forty-eight hours."

I grumble as he slides off the bed, making it impossible for me to reach for his belt and try to force myself upon him. "Fine. Fine. I'll go," I say, giving in to him. "But just so you know…" I stand near the edge of the bed and adjust my shirt. "I may not be in the mood on Friday."

"The mood?" he asks.

"For dick, baby."

His laugh is loud and immediate. "Still a shit liar. You're always in the mood."

That statement earns him two middle fingers. "We'll see."

He reaches out, gripping my hip with his massive hand, digging those fingertips into the flesh just above my waistband. "You know you can never say no."

"I can too," I say, but my voice cracks, betraying the hell out of me.

"You're not going to get me to change my mind. The sun is on the way down, and if you wait any longer, it'll be too dangerous for you to go. Eagle and Ginger will look after me while I'm here."

I move as slow as molasses as I toe on my sandals. "I'm pretty sure those guys are already shit-faced."

Mammoth stalks toward me until his shadow

covers me and he blocks out the overhead light. "I'm just going to sleep. I'm exhausted after the last few days and could really use a good night's sleep to get my head on straight."

"You sleep so much better with me curled next to you."

He smiles. "I love how relentless you are."

"Only when it comes to you."

"You're dragging your feet, princess. It's time to go. I'll see you in two days."

I wrap my arm around his middle and place my head on his chest, listening to the steady, strong beat of his heart. A few days ago, I was petrified he'd die. Even now, standing here, it's my greatest fear. "Promise me you'll be careful."

"I promise," he whispers against my hair as I breathe in the scent of his T-shirt and memorize his warmth.

The heat of his body is gone a moment later. "Let's get you in your car."

"Can we go out the back door?" I ask him. "I don't want to walk through the bar area and see the guys."

I'm not in the mood, holding each of them partially responsible for Mammoth being alone and vulnerable when he was shot. I know they aren't to blame, but petty is my middle name and grudges are something I can hold a lifetime.

"Whatever you want," he says.

"I want to stay," I mutter under my breath.

But in under sixty seconds, we're standing in the parking lot of the compound, my ass resting against the driver's door of my car.

"Call me when you get to your apartment and make it inside," he tells me, running his knuckles down my cheek. "I want to know you're safe."

"Why don't you just come with me? I have my own place this year."

He shakes his head. "I have shit to tie up here before I can get gone for good."

I sigh. "Then come to my place tomorrow."

He wraps his fingers around my upper arms, squeezing me gently. "Baby, I'll be a distraction, and I need to get my ass moving on the garage. By the time you graduate, I want the place to be remodeled, operating, and making money. I can't lie around your apartment all day while you go to class. It's not me. I wasn't built to do nothing."

"But you'd look so good on my couch."

"How about this…" He strokes the skin on the back of my arm with his fingertips, giving me goose bumps even in the heat. "I'll come visit you some weekends instead of you driving so far all the time."

"No way. I can't miss my grandmother's dinner on Sunday, and I need to see my family too. So, while that's super sweet of you, that's a negative, sparky."

"Sparky?" He furrows his eyebrows.

I shrug. "It's better than baby. You look like a sparky."

"Give me your lips before you go," he says, his voice deep and gravelly.

Without hesitation, I lift myself up on my tiptoes and tilt my head back to offer him my mouth like I've offered everything else to him in the past.

One of his hands leaves my arm and moves to the back of my head, tugging on my hair. "I love you, princess."

"Love you too, sparky." I smile as his lips crash down on mine, stealing my breath again. I memorize the taste of his lips, the softness of his tongue, the forcefulness of his mouth.

He'll be okay.

He's alive.

He's safe.

I repeat those words to myself as he kisses me, remembering how very lucky we are the bullet didn't hit a few inches over, finding his heart.

"Bye," I whisper when he pulls away and reaches behind me for the handle of my car door.

"I'll be waiting for your call."

I nod, holding back the tears as I curl into the driver's seat. I will not cry. I'm not a crier. I never have been and never will be. But if anyone could bring me to the brink, it's him. Damn JD

Saint and all of his manliness for making me weak.

He shuts the door and waves me goodbye as I back out, my eyes going from the cement to him until he is nothing but a speck in the rearview mirror.

He is fine.

I am fine.

We'll be fine.

THE COMPOUND REEKS of stale cigarettes and cheap beer as I stalk through the sea of bodies.

"Mammoth!" Eagle yells across the room, rising from his spot on the couch next to his newest piece of ass. "Fuckin' finally, man. Where the hell have you been? Texted you hours ago."

"Yo." I lift my chin as I jam my keys into my pocket, trying to hide my disgust about being back here. "I went out for a ride in the truck to clear my head after Tamara left."

"I've been sitting here saving a cold beer for you."

"You sure about that?" I tick my head toward the half-dressed woman he just left. "Looks like you were busy with that brunette."

"Eh, you know I prefer blondes." He gives me a

toothy grin, nudging me with his elbow. "But my best friend beats cheap pussy any day."

I lift an eyebrow, knowing he's full of shit.

"Okay. Maybe you don't *always* trump pussy—" he throws his thumb over his shoulder, pointing to the brown-haired woman who looks more like road trash than a runway model "—but you beat *that* piece of ass."

I slap him on the shoulder, laughing. "I feel special. Thanks, man."

"You should, asshole. The bitch doesn't have real teeth."

My eyebrows furrow as I stare at him in confusion. She doesn't have real teeth. What in the actual fuck? "Sounds tragic."

"Dude, you don't know what you're missing. Gum jobs are the best fuckin' shit ever."

I blink, wondering if I heard him wrong but knowing I didn't. "A gum job?" I cringe as my stomach rolls at the very thought, picturing her popping out her dentures to suck his cock.

He stares me straight in the eyes and taps his finger against my chest. "You haven't lived until you've had one. Trust me, brother."

Somehow, I hold back the vomit climbing up my throat. "You're really fucked up."

His smile widens. "Was there ever any doubt?"

"None," I deadpan as Morris comes to stand beside us.

"I'll take one of those." Morris motions toward Eagle's beer.

"Morris, I need you," Ginger says from behind us. "There's someone at the door."

Morris glares at Ginger. "Who?"

"A woman." Ginger shrugs, looking like he's about to run. "She wouldn't give a name. She's just standing outside, shaking."

"Pussy is nothing but a headache," he tells me, knocking his knuckles against the bar top before he brushes past Ginger, leaving us alone.

I tip my head back, staring up at the ceiling. "Total asshole," I whisper to no one but myself.

Eagle pushes my beer bottle closer. "Stop pouting like a little bitch and drink up."

"Fuck off with that bullshit," I tell him as I grab the beer, guzzling.

"I can make you a spot of tea if you prefer," Eagle teases. "Now that you're fancy and shit."

I give him my middle finger as I take another drink.

"Didn't think so. This is my last night to drink with my best friend, and we're going to do it right."

"It's not like we'll never see each other again."

He raises an eyebrow.

"You're family, man. You're welcome in my home anytime," I reassure him.

"Would Tamara say the same?" he asks.

"She would. She likes you for some crazy-ass reason I'll never understand."

He leans forward, beer in hand, resting his arm against the bar. "She's a good woman. You're making the right choice. This—" he waves his hand in front of us to the room filled with drunken fools "—was never meant to be your life."

"I don't deserve a woman like her."

Eagle straightens. "You're the best of the best, Mammoth. Don't let memories mess with your head."

"I've done some bad shit."

He places his hand on my good shoulder, squeezing. "You don't go out of your way looking for trouble. We all make choices in life. Some good. Some bad. Shit happens. We move on." Eagle's dark eyes bore into me as he holds my gaze. "And it's time for you to move on."

I try to soak in his words and believe what he's saying is true. "It's not that easy."

"Hey," he says, slapping me lightly across the face. "I've never lied to you, and I'm not about to start now. You get as far away from this place as you can, and never look back. You hear me?"

When I came to the Disciples, I needed them. I didn't feel like I had a purpose after leaving the service. I was a boat without a rudder, wandering on an endless sea of nothingness. "Yeah, man."

"We've all done shit we're not proud of. Put it behind you. Ball it up tight and stuff it so deep you never feel or think about it again. Do you think those jagoffs would even give you a second thought if you were buried in the ground?"

I draw in a deep breath and close my eyes. "They would not."

"Damn fuckin' right, they wouldn't. They wouldn't feel remorse or sadness. They would've spat on your grave and danced around your corpse. Don't you forget that shit either."

"You're right," I grumble, not wanting to admit those words even if they are true.

"Imagine if you would've died and what that would've done to your woman."

My chest tightens. Tamara would've been a mess. For all her sass and attitude, she has the softest heart and would've been forever changed by my death. I know this.

"I could use another drink," I tell him, wanting nothing more than to change the subject and lose myself for a night.

"About damn time." Eagle smiles, and the wrinkles near his eyes deepen. "I thought you'd gone completely soft on me."

"Old man, the only thing soft between the two of us is your dick."

"It may be soft, but it's still big enough you'd choke on it."

I laugh. "I'm going to miss your dumb ass. You sure you don't want to leave this place and join me?"

He bends, reaching underneath to the small fridge, and comes up with two cold beers. "Like retire?" he asks, sliding one of the bottles toward me. "Do I look like I'm ready to retire?"

I shake my head as I twist off the cap. "Not retire, but finally live. I'm opening a garage over there. You're good with cars and bikes. I could use a partner."

His eyes sparkle for a moment and I think he's going to bite, but then he opens his mouth and says, "I'm not ready for that yet." He leans against the bar, taking a small swig of beer. "I have a lot of miles left to travel and a lot of unfinished business to clear off my plate before I can settle down in a small town and grow old."

"When you're ready, I'll have a place for you," I promise him, wanting him to know he always has an out if he wants it.

But Eagle is a lifer.

His father was in the brotherhood until he took his last breath, and Eagle has wanted nothing more than to follow in his footsteps.

"I appreciate that. If I change my mind, you'll be the first one to know."

"Yo, Mammoth!" Morris calls out across the room from the entrance. "Get your ass over here."

I roll my eyes at Eagle, who chuckles with a shrug. "What the hell does he want now?" I grumble.

"Fuck if I know."

"Goddamn it. Why me?" I ask, setting down my beer on the bar before heading toward Morris.

Morris has his arms folded in front of his chest, shoulders pushed back, a pinched expression on his face. "I don't know why all your broads feel like they can just show up here unannounced."

My gaze moves toward the open door behind him. "Tam's here?"

Morris shakes his head. "A different one."

I furrow my brows, knowing there's no other broad in my life except Tamara. "Different?" I stop walking, moving my eyes back to Morris.

He nods, shrugging a shoulder. "Fuckin' pussy magnet. I'll never understand it."

As I start walking toward him again, he backs away from the door, making room for me. "You need to get a better handle on your bitches," he tells me. "Remind them who's boss."

I step toward the doorway, ignoring his asshole comment.

The woman's head is bowed as she stares at the

cement underneath her feet, hearing our entire conversation.

My heart stops when I see the soft wave of her brown hair and her tiny frame. It's been years since I've laid eyes on her, but she's unmistakable.

"Mom?"

CHAPTER SEVEN

MAMMOTH

"I DIDN'T KNOW where else to go," Mom says, her eyes filled with tears as she peers up at me.

My chest burns and my stomach tightens as I pull her into my arms without a second thought. "What happened? Whatever it is, I'll help."

"I can't…" she whispers, not finishing the statement as her fingers curl into the soft cotton of my T-shirt. "It's nothing. Really. I shouldn't have come here." She starts to push herself away. "I hate to be a bother."

I pull back, tipping my head down, forcing her to look at me like she used to do when I was a kid, as I tighten my grip on her. "This isn't nothing, Ma, and we're going to talk about whatever this is," I tell her, moving her inside the compound's main room and closing the door. "You're never a bother. You're my mother, and I love you."

Her eyes widen as her gaze moves across the room. The naked bodies. The drunken men. The bar slash strip club atmosphere only a biker clubhouse in the evening can have.

"JD," she whispers, her body stiffening. "This is where you live?" Mom has never been one to judge, but I can hear it in her tone. She's judging, and I'm guilty as hell too.

I know how it looks.

I know what she's thinking without her saying the words.

"It's not as bad as it looks, Ma. I swear. You just caught us on a bad night," I reassure her, lying my ass off because it's exactly how it looks, no matter how much I want to deny it.

She blinks as she gazes up at me in disbelief. "Not as bad as it looks?" she asks softly. "There're naked women everywhere."

I smile, biting back my laughter because I'm not about to give my mom lip, especially since she came here because she needed something. "Let's go to my room and talk. Away from all this sin."

She nods, placing her hand in mine before I pull her toward the hallway near the back. She nearly trips a few times, too busy gawking at the people around us instead of looking where she's walking.

I don't stop moving until we're at my door, and I fish a key from my pocket.

"Why do you lock your door?" she asks, always full of questions. "Is it that unsafe here?"

"I trust the guys, but not the women."

She sucks in a breath. "Are *they* here often?"

I work on the lock, not bothering with eye contact because she's always been able to read my face. "No, not often. Tonight is just…" I pause as I turn the knob. "Special."

She follows me inside, spinning around the room as she soaks in the place I've been living for the last six years.

She's never come here before. I wasn't even sure she knew exactly where I've been until tonight.

"The room is nice," she says, but her nose is wrinkled.

"Sit," I tell her, moving her by the shoulders to the end of my bed before she gets us sidetracked. "We're not leaving until you tell me everything." I kneel before her, peering up at her and studying the small changes in her face since the last time I saw her. "Tell me what happened."

Her blue eyes meet mine, searching my face. "Promise me you won't get mad."

I grunt, tightening my hands into fists. "I promise," I lie.

If I get mad, it won't be with her. No doubt this

has to do with some dumb-ass guy or one of her bitch-ass girlfriends.

Someone did her wrong, and whoever they are, they are going to pay.

She reaches out, pressing her palms to my face, giving me a sad smile. "You look tired, baby."

I place my hands over hers. "Ma, don't change the subject. Talk to me," I beg her again.

Tipping her head forward, she rests her forehead against mine and closes her eyes. "I met this man a few months ago."

My teeth grind together, but I keep my mouth shut. She's finally talking, and I'm not letting my anger stop her. I think I know where this is going, and I prep myself for words I don't want to hear.

Her blue eyes meet my gray ones with our faces only a few inches apart. "He was great. Super sweet and caring. Went out of his way to do nice things for me. He was protective and thoughtful. Everything I'd been wanting and couldn't find in a person since your father died."

I blow out a breath and soften my features, knowing this isn't easy for her. The least I can do is not scowl while she spills her guts.

"A few weeks ago, he asked to borrow some money." She draws in a breath and closes her eyes again like whatever she's about to say is too painful to do while looking at me. "I told him no because it wasn't a small amount, and even though I had feelings for him, I didn't feel comfortable saying yes."

"It's your money, Ma. You have every right to do what you want with it, including telling him no."

"Boyd wasn't happy with my answer. He told me he wouldn't have asked if it weren't important. I still told him no and not to ask me again."

"Good. You stuck to your guns."

I was proud of her. She'd never been a pushover. Being a single mother made her stronger than most, and she never put up with anyone's shit, not even from a man.

"That was the first time he hit me," she whispers.

I see red.

Not just red, but blood red.

All the air evaporates from my lungs, and the burn in my chest is something I haven't felt quite so deep for a long time. Then her words really slam into me. The first time…meaning he did it more than once, but this is the first time I'm hearing about it.

"I will bury him."

Her eyes snap open, and her hands on my face tighten as she pulls her head back to look at me. "No, you will not, Josiah."

Her calling me by my first name doesn't change the simple fact—he will feel a pain worse than he ever inflicted on my mother. No man lays a hand on a woman, especially not the one who gave birth to me. "Ma…"

Her eyes narrow, and the tears that have started to form spill over onto her cheeks. "You will not touch him."

"Ma…"

She shakes her head. "I handled him."

My brows furrow as I stare at her, blinking. "You handled him?" I whisper.

She nods as she wipes at her face. "I made sure he'll think twice before he lays a hand on another woman. That's why I had to leave, and I couldn't think of anywhere safe to go but to come here."

"You should've left the first time he hit you, Ma."

Fuck.

She always taught me never to lay hands on a woman, but she took that blow and stayed for another.

"I was stupid. I believed him when he apologized and said he didn't mean to touch me. I bought the lie. I did what women do when they want to believe the best of a person even though they're faced with the worst."

"At least you got away free and clear."

She cringes and rocks backward on the edge of my bed. "I'm on the run, baby."

I rock back on my heels and freeze.

She was hit more than once.

She took care of it herself.

She's on the run.

All words I never thought I'd hear my mother say, but here she is, saying them.

"I'll take care of it," I promise her.

Her eyes widen. "It's not an easy fix. You know small towns. He has friends on the city council. The entire police force is looking for me."

I grunt. Small-town police forces are a joke. They are easily bought, and I have enough money to probably buy them all. "I already told you, I'll take care of it, Ma."

"But I…" She pauses and runs her small fingers across her forehead. "I…"

"Tell me what happened," I ask softly.

"The last time he hit me—" She stops again and grimaces.

She just said the last time he hit her, but she didn't say the second time. That means this shit was going on for a while, and yet she never called me to clue me in. She should've left after the first time or at least made a phone call, telling me what was happening so I could make sure he never touched her, or any woman, ever again.

"The last time he hit me, I went into the garage while he was sleeping and grabbed the sledgehammer."

This isn't going anywhere pretty, but I already

have a sense of pride bubbling deep inside me. No one grabs a sledgehammer unless they plan to use it. The weight and force of something so big is not a match for the frailty of the human body.

"I walked into the house, tiptoeing into the living room where he was lying on the couch, and I lifted the hammer as high as I could before I brought that bitch down on the arm he used to strike me."

Somehow, I don't move a muscle, keeping my face impartial and not trying to seem as shocked as I feel. "He deserved that and worse."

She nods with a small smile, the first glimmer of radiance coming off her. A sliver of the Ma I saw last time I laid eyes on her. "I'm not a violent person, Josiah. You know this, but I couldn't take it anymore. I didn't see another way out. I had to make it impossible for him to hit me again."

"You did that," I say with a hint of laughter.

Mom literally brought down the hammer on the asshole.

"I never saw a man scream the way he did. There was so much blood, baby. So much blood." Her face pales as she stares at the door behind me, unable to make eye contact. "And the sound. Oh my God. The sound bone makes when it breaks is the most horrific… And then when it tore through his skin…" She pales.

"Ma," I say, bringing her back to the here and

now instead of staying in her memories. "You're here. You're safe. And you did the right thing."

"I have a lot of forgiveness to ask for and prayers to say. I don't think there's enough penance to make up for my actions this time, sweetheart."

I shake my head, gripping her hands with mine. "He's the one who needs to ask for forgiveness, Ma, not you. You were protecting yourself. Plain as that."

"He was sleeping," she whispers.

"Did he hit you?"

"Yes."

"Then he deserved it. I don't care what the hell he was doing when you hit him, you did the right thing."

"So, now…" She sighs, hanging her head. "I'm on the run with a warrant out for my arrest." She squirms as she says the words, and the lines in her face deepen. "You were the first person to pop in my head, and I figured this was probably the one place the cops wouldn't be looking for me."

"You did the right thing coming here." I climb to my feet, releasing her hand as I do. "The club will protect you, and you can stay here." But fuck, this adds another layer of complication I hadn't anticipated, just when I was ready to leave.

She tips her head back, gawking at me as her brown hair spills down her back. "You want me to stay here?"

I nod, rubbing the back of my neck. "No safer place to be when the law is looking for you."

"But…"

I shake my head, putting my hand out in front of me. "It's not up for discussion."

She snaps her mouth shut, eyes going wide. I've never talked to her this way, and it shows in the shock on her face.

"You're staying here. If you need something, one of the guys will get it. But for the time being, until I can get shit sorted, you do not go outside the gates."

Her nose scrunches. "I can't stay here with those —" she waves her hand toward the door "—naked people," she whispers.

"The women don't live here. They come and go. The guys are going to keep your ass out of jail and alive, Ma. I want no lip."

Her head jerks back, and her eyes flash with anger. "I think you forget who the parent is here, Josiah."

"I haven't forgotten. You came to me for help, and I'm doing that." I move toward the door and open it, finding Eagle walking down the hallway. "Grab Morris, will ya?"

"Sure thing, brother. Everything okay in there?" He tries to look over my shoulder, knowing damn well there's a woman in my room.

I'm sure word has already spread that she's my

mother. I can see questions swimming through his brain. Ones he won't ask and shit I don't have time to answer right now.

"Everything's fine. Just get him," I bark.

Eagle gives me a nod before stalking toward the common room, keeping all his questions to himself.

"Who's Morris?" Ma asks, fidgeting with the hem of her dress near her knees.

"He's the one who answered the door."

"Oh," she whispers, gazing down. "He seemed…*nice*. Is he your boss?"

"He's the club's VP."

"So, I take it he's kind of a big deal, then?"

I laugh softly, loving her naïveté about motorcycle clubs. "He is a big deal, but don't ever tell him I said that."

"Heard that shit. Never forgetting it," Morris says as he comes through the doorway to my bedroom without even so much as a knock. "No taking it back."

I sigh, growling under my breath. "Close the door," I tell him as he stands there, his gaze moving from me to my mother.

He does as I ask without a smartass response before crossing his arms, looking mean as hell and curious as ever, leaning against the wall.

"Morris." I wave my hand toward my mother, who's still sitting on the bed and looking at him with the widest eyes. "This is my mother, Jessica."

"Ma'am," he says, unfolding those burly arms to rub the back of his neck. "Nice to formally meet you."

"You too," she whispers, the deer in headlights look still firmly planted on her face. "Sir."

Morris's lips twitch at that comment, and by the way he's looking at Mom, I already want to claw his eyes out. "Morris, please."

"Now that the introductions are out of the way, Morris, I need your help. She needs your help."

"You know I always got your back, brother. Your mom's too, for that matter."

"I'm wanted by the cops," she blurts out.

"Interesting," he mumbles, moving toward her and then pacing between us. "Misdemeanor?"

"Felony," she tells him.

His eyes widen, and then his face softens a second later. "That's some pretty heavy shit for a little thing like you."

She nods, watching him as he starts to pace. "I didn't mean for it to happen."

I stare at her, trying to hold back my laughter at her statement because grabbing a sledgehammer and using it on a man is no accident. My mom has always had the patience of a saint, but everybody has a breaking point, even her.

"Do you mind me asking what happened?" he says as he comes to a stop in front of her, ignoring me.

She nods. "I'll tell you whatever you want to know."

He bends forward and takes a knee a few feet away from her, studying her face. "How deep are you, sugar?"

"Sugar?" she whispers and blushes.

I roll my eyes and growl. Is he really hitting on my mother while I'm standing there watching? That shit is never going to happen as long as I'm still breathing.

Morris peers over his shoulder, drawing his bushy eyebrows down, telling me in his subtle way to calm my shit and keep my mouth shut.

I take a seat across the room as I let him continue, but in no way am I leaving. "Go on," I tell him when he doesn't give his attention back to her.

"Mr. Morris, I really didn't mean to do it," she whispers, propping her elbows on her knees and dropping her cheeks to her palms. "I've made a mess of everything."

"We'll clean it up. Tell me whatever you feel comfortable with, and I'll find out the rest on my own," he says softly, almost comforting her.

I knew he was the one to call in here. Morris is tough and can be the biggest asshole in the world, but I know women are his weakness. He shows as much with Gigi and Tamara. He loves those girls and makes sure no one lays a hand on them or gets out of line when they are around.

"I was seeing this guy."

Morris grunts, probably thinking he knows where this is going, but he is about to be thrown for a big fucking loop. "Go on."

"He hit me a few times…"

Morris's back straightens as his body stiffens.

Hearing the words a second time doesn't make it any easier for me either. The very thought of someone laying their hands on my mother…he's going to wish for another blow from a sledgehammer instead of what I have planned for him.

"No man should ever hit a woman," Morris tells her with his arm lying across his propped-up knee, staying relaxed and calm. "That's unacceptable, Ms. Saint. Whatever you did, I'm sure you were one hundred percent justified."

"I may have gone to the extreme." She smiles softly.

"Sometimes the only way to fight violence is with violence. Did you shoot him?"

Mom shakes her head. "Oh God, no. I don't even own a gun."

That is something we are going to fix. I am going to buy her one and teach her how to shoot it. She needs protection, especially living alone. And if some asshole ever decides to lay his hands on her again, she can quickly put an end to it.

"Well." He tilts his head, studying her. "I don't see you packing that much of a punch."

I lean forward, waiting for the moment she tells him what she did because I know he's about to have his mind freaking blown.

"I used a sledgehammer on him."

Morris rocks backward at that little revelation. "Well, shit, sugar. That takes some balls." He laughs, and my mom's serious face breaks for a moment.

"I didn't know what else to do, but it wasn't right of me."

He touches her leg, and I force myself to stay seated. "I hope you broke more than a few bones," he says, shaking his head. "The man deserved as much and worse."

"There was so much blood," she whispers. "I think there was definitely more than one bone broken."

"Sounds like a damn good swing you have." He laughs.

Mom laughs too. "It'll be a long time before he can throw another right hook."

Morris sobers, and the burn in my belly deepens, growing molten. "He punched you?"

Mom nods as her eyes drop down, and her smile dies. "First, he slapped me, but the next few times, it was a closed fist."

Morris sucks in a breath as I shoot out of my

chair, ready to find the guy and murder him on the spot. Don't give two shits if I spend a lifetime behind bars; the asshole deserves a very slow and painful death.

"Sit," Morris barks, talking to me but not glancing my way.

Mom's eyes meet mine, and I can see the shame and sadness behind the blue. Something I've never seen grace her face in all my years of breathing.

"Ms. Saint, we'll protect you, and we'll handle the asshole and make sure you never have to worry about him or the cops again."

"You are very kind," she whispers. "This isn't your problem, though. I made this mess. I should just turn myself in."

He lifts his hand, silencing her. "Mammoth is our family, and now, so are you. We take care of family. We look out for one another. We keep one another safe. You're one of us now. There's no other place in the world you should be except here."

"But…"

"Want a drink?" he asks her, stopping whatever she was going to say.

She nods. "I could really use some whiskey."

"You got it." He smiles at her as he stands. "I'll clear the clubhouse, and we'll drink."

"Oh, don't go to all that trouble. It looked like

everyone was having a *nice* time. I hate to be the reason to ruin everyone's night."

"Ma'am, family always comes before pussy."

Mom blanches at his frank statement, but it's always been the truth, however crude the words. "Well, okay," she says softly, eyes moving to me as I nod.

Morris marches toward me. "Give me five, and bring her out."

"You sure? I can keep her…"

Morris shakes his head. "Five and then at the bar. Both of you need a fucking drink, and we need a goddamn plan."

CHAPTER EIGHT

TAMARA

"PRINCESS," Mammoth says, finally calling me hours after I sent him a text message.

"Babe. What the fuck?" I ask.

"What the fuck?" he repeats.

"Yeah. What the actual fuck? I texted you hours ago. How hard is it to text back and say you're busy?"

"Well, I—"

"No. I don't want to hear another excuse," I cut him off from telling me some bullshit. "It takes two seconds to type 'I'm busy,' so I know you're not dead somewhere, no longer breathing."

"Tam."

"Mammoth, I'm dead fucking serious. I've been here, pacing the floors like a wild animal and thinking the absolute worst. I was about to drive back to the compound."

"I'm sorry, princess."

"I never used to worry, but ever since…" I draw in a deep breath, hearing his growl on the other end. "Just take a few seconds so I don't prematurely age from stress. Got it? Because right now, I'm so pissed…"

"My mom's here," he blurts out in the middle of my chewing him a new asshole.

I stop moving and scrunch my face. "Your mom?"

"She just showed up out of nowhere and knocked on the door. At first, I thought you were back, being all cute, not following directions."

It wouldn't be the first time I just showed up at the massive steel doors of the Disciples, looking for someone. But I'm trying to be better and more in control of my actions and my mind, not letting myself assume the worst every moment of every day.

"But then I saw her, and it was like someone sucker-punched me right in the gut."

"Is she okay?"

"She is now, but she wasn't. She's in some shit, and if anyone shows up asking for her, you don't know where she is."

"Whatever you want and need me to say, sparky."

"You know nothing."

I nod to myself. "What am I supposed to know?"

"Good. I won't be heading back tomorrow. I need

to stay here and sort shit out with her. She got into some trouble, and she's hiding from the cops."

Well, okay. Those aren't the words I thought he was going to tell me. From everything I know about her, she doesn't seem like the criminal type. "Bring her here. I can hide her," I offer.

"No. She has to stay at the compound with the guys until I get shit straightened out."

Oh boy. From what Mammoth has told me, she isn't much of a party girl and likes to attend church regularly. I'm pretty damn sure being surrounded by a bunch of dirty-ass bikers will be a bit of a culture shock.

"Want me to come back and keep her company?" I ask, hating that he pushed me out the door.

"Let me sleep on it. It's been a long day, and I'll be thinking more clearly in the morning, yeah? Just go to class and at least see what you missed."

"Yeah," I whisper. "I can do that."

"She's pretty upset right now, and she's not sure about the guys. I'm sure she'd rather spend time with you, but I need to get my head straight and figure out what we're going to do before I make any decisions."

"She shouldn't be sure about them," I say, laughing on the other end, picturing her meeting Morris, Tiny, and the guys covered in tattoos, facial hair, and leather. Totally isn't Jessica's scene, and she probably feels like a fish out of water right now.

"You know what. Can you come after class tomorrow? I wouldn't feel right leaving her at the compound without me."

"Someone have their eye on her already?" I tease him.

"Morris was a little too sweet."

"Ah. You don't trust him around her?"

"He trusted me with you, and look how that turned out."

I bite my lip, trying to stop myself from laughing. "Point taken. I'll head your way tomorrow after my last class."

"Bring some shit for a few days if you can."

"Done. I'll see what I'm going to miss on Friday, so I don't fall further behind."

"Also, can you grab some clothes and whatever women use for my mom? She showed up with nothing except the clothes on her back."

"Sure. What does she like to wear?"

"She likes sundresses, and she's a size small. Maybe a robe and a pair of pajamas. You know, the ugly kind with the matching pants."

I roll my eyes. "I got it. I'll bring her some toiletries too."

"I hate asking you to do all this, but I don't want to ask the—"

"Don't you dare ask those skanky bitches."

He laughs for the first time during our conversation. "They're not all bad."

"You're right, but they're not trustworthy," I concede, even though it almost kills me. "But I'll take care of your mom. No one else. Got it?"

"Got it. I gotta go. Sleep well, princess, and I'll see you tomorrow."

"Love you."

"Love you too," he says before disconnecting.

I'M BARELY awake as I grab a cup of coffee from the kitchen and stalk toward the bar area to have a seat. But when I walk into the main room, I'm not alone…and neither is my mother.

Morris is next to her, body turned, knee touching the side of her thigh. They're talking, and he's full of smiles, while she watches him in sheer fascination.

"Fucking bullshit," I mutter into my mug as a growl climbs up my throat, escaping before I take my first sip.

I catch Morris's eye, and he quickly shifts his body into a new position.

Smart.

"Mornin'," Morris says, acting like I didn't just see what I saw. Words will be had, but not until we're alone so I don't embarrass my mother.

Ma turns to face me with a small smile still on her lips. "Morning, baby," she says as she slides off the stool and walks toward me. "Sleep well?"

"Ma," I tell her, shaking my head. "You can't call me baby here."

She looks around the empty room, no one but her and Morris there with me because everyone else is either busy working or not awake. "Why?" She looks so innocent when she asks the question.

"It's just not cool."

She laughs, her blue eyes sparkling. "You mean it's not manly?"

I nod. "Something like that."

She turns back toward Morris, who's laughing his ass off behind his hand. "Morris, can I call you baby?"

"Sugar, you can call me anything you like, but I have a feeling your boy wouldn't like it too much."

I can't stop myself from glaring at Morris, but I quickly wipe the look off my face when Ma glances at me again.

"Would you care if I called him baby?"

"It's different, and I sure as fuck would care," I tell her, careful to control the volume of my voice. No matter how old I am, she's still my mom and will not hesitate to put my ass in place.

"Language," she warns me like I'm ten again.

I glance up to the ceiling, muttering a slew of curse words under my breath.

"Josiah," Ma whispers, touching my chest. "I didn't even know you knew all those words, and the fact that you'd say them in front of me is even more shocking."

I tip my face down to the tiny woman who gave me life. "I'm sorry. This is just so awkward, Ma. I'm used to just being me when I'm here. I can't act like a church boy just because you're around."

"Hold up." Morris lifts his hand, shifting his body in our direction. "You were an altar boy?"

I give him the middle finger, careful so my mother doesn't see. "Ma, this is my home. These are my people. They swear. They don't hold back. They don't attend mass. And they never refer to me as Josiah or baby. I don't think Morris even knew that was my first name. Here, I'm Mammoth."

"I knew about Josiah," he interjects, holding up a finger. "Background check."

I roll my eyes. "Whatever, Morris."

"Be nice, Josiah," Ma says, tapping her finger against my chest, my name sounding so foreign coming off her tongue. "Morris has been a complete gentleman, and you've done nothing but throw him attitude this morning."

I stare down at her, holding the cup of coffee in

my hand as it cools with each passing second. "Can I drink this?"

Her eyes move from the cup to her side. "Come and sit with us."

"Yes." Morris pats the stool next to him. "We have a lot to talk about with Jessica."

As Ma starts to walk away, I notice she's no longer in the sundress from last night, but a big T-shirt and a pair of sweatpants that I didn't give her. "Where did you get those clothes?"

"Morris gave them to me," she says without turning around.

My gaze moves to him, and he shrugs. "I found them in my room, buried in a drawer. She couldn't wear the same clothes two days in a row." His words are code for: one of the bitches he fucked in the past left them behind.

I slide onto the stool next to Morris where my mother had been and move her coffee to my left, away from him. "Tamara's bringing you some dresses later today. You won't have to stay in that ridiculous outfit for long."

"I was sitting there," she says to my back as she stands behind me, not sitting in the spot I've made for her.

"Well, now you're sitting there." I point to her coffee, making sure she knows I'm not moving. "So, sit there."

She grunts, but a moment later, she's next to me just like I told her. "I'm not sure I like this side of you."

"I only have one side."

"Jessica, sugar," Morris says, leaning forward to see her and ignoring me again. "Let's talk about the man and what happened. Do you feel comfortable telling us more? I need names, dates, details."

I grind my teeth together, keeping the burning in my stomach from roaring out of my throat and saying something I know I'll regret.

Mom nods, tucking a lock of her brown hair behind her ear. "His name is Boyd Weaver. We had mutual friends and all, so I figured he was a good guy. One night, he saw me out at a festival and asked me to dinner." She pauses, staring down at her half-empty coffee.

"Okay." Morris nods. "Then what?"

"We dated for a few months. Everything was great. He seemed like the perfect man. Kind, caring, and considerate. He was so attentive."

"They always seem like the greatest guys," Morris replies, and I sip my coffee, trying to keep myself busy to divert the rage building in me toward Boyd Weaver.

"Around the fourth month, I sold my house and moved in with him."

I snap my head to the side, and my eyes widen. "You sold the house?"

"You know, bab…Mammoth—" she places her hand on my arm "—I never get attached to places. They are always temporary."

"But you sank everything you had into that place and said you'd spend the rest of your life watching the sunsets from the back porch."

She shrugs with a frown. "I thought I'd found a different future."

Her words are like a punch to the gut. A gutless bastard not only laid his hands on my mother, but he convinced her to sell her dream. If he isn't dying by bleeding out from the sledgehammer, he is going to by my hand.

"Keep going, Jessica," Morris tells her as he lifts his hand, placing it on my shoulder and squeezing.

I turn my head, glaring at Morris, and he gives me a nod and a look I know far too well. It's a situation we're going to handle. Why does he have any skin in the game? I don't know. Maybe it's out of loyalty to me, even in a time when I want nothing more to do with the club. Either way, I know I'm no longer on my own.

"I don't want to get into all the details. I told you enough last night. Finally, I had enough and took it upon myself to make sure he could never use that hand on me again. I got in my car and drove, leaving everything behind."

"I can run a background check on Boyd, but it

would be faster if you tell us what you know about him. Where he's from, where he lives, the work he's done in the past or still does. Anything you can tell us to understand the man before we head up north."

Her eyes grow wide. "You can't go north."

"Like hell, we can't," Morris says, not giving me a chance.

"You show up, scared and shaking. You bet your ass, your son and I are going to take a little trip and make sure this asshole gets what he deserves."

I curl my hand into a fist against the wood of the bar top. "We'll make sure you're cleared of the charges too, Ma." I know that's what is really on her mind. She's worried about the law coming after her and not Boyd, but men who abuse women are rarely so quick to let them go.

She slides her hand over my fist. "I only care about the charges."

"We'll make that happen," I promise her.

"It's not that easy. Boyd used to be a cop. He has connections, and he's on the city council. You two aren't going to be able to make a few calls and get this swept under the rug."

Morris laughs. "Sugar," he says, pausing before he clears his throat, so he doesn't look like the asshole he is. "I don't care if he has all the connections in the world. We have our own. A man who hits women doesn't get to hide behind his connections or his old badge either."

"Boyd has a small arsenal inside his home. It's too dangerous for you two to go after him. I wanted to get away, and I did that. I took him by surprise and had my keys ready. The last thing I want is to invite him back in by having you going up there, stirring up more trouble."

I side-eye Morris, and he nods.

"We won't do anything unless it's necessary," he tells her.

In the Disciples, revenge is always necessary. An eye for an eye is woven into the fabric of this club. Making peace, while it can be useful, doesn't come without someone paying a price first.

Boyd Weaver is in for a world of hurt.

***

"Tam!" the guys yell when Tamara walks through the front door, carrying a giant white shopping bag.

Eagle's quick to take it from her hands before I have a chance to make it halfway across the room, leaving my mother with Morris.

"Thanks, Eagle."

He nods to Tamara before making eye contact with me as he stalks back across the room to my mother.

"Princess, I've never been so happy to see your face." My hands find her ass, and I hold her tight.

She throws her arms around me and smashes her lips to mine. "Sorry I wasn't here earlier. My professor didn't want to stop talking," she murmurs against my mouth, smelling like sunshine and everything sweet.

"I'm just glad you're here now. Don't apologize."

She tilts her head toward the bar, eyes narrowing. "What's up with that?"

I sigh and close my eyes. "Morris is cozying up to my mother, or maybe she's cozying up to him. Whatever it is, I don't like it."

Tam laughs and pats my chest. "It's just Morris being Morris. I wouldn't worry about anything. I mean, your mom isn't really old lady material or a side piece of ass."

I grumble under my breath. "Did you think you'd still be here with me?"

Tamara bites her lip. "Well, I always had a wild side, baby. Your mama wouldn't know wild if it hit her in the face."

I grimace.

"What?"

"Her boyfriend was beating her."

Tamara rocks back, eyes as big as saucers. "He was what?"

I nod. "It's why she's here. She took matters into

her own hands, and the slimy bastard had the balls to call the cops on her."

She blinks. "What?"

"Yeah."

"Wait. So, he hit her, but the cops want her?"

I nod again. "He used to be a cop."

"That doesn't make sense. Why would they want her?"

"She had enough and made him pay. Now there's a warrant out for her."

Her face twists. "Did you call James and Thomas?"

"Didn't even think about it yet."

"You call them. They'll set that shit right."

"All right. I'll do that tomorrow. Morris and I are going to take a little trip to visit her ex too."

Tamara takes a step back and crosses her arms over her chest, dropping one shoulder. "You're going to do what?"

"Princess, don't get upset."

She raises an eyebrow. "You're telling me you're going to go give payback to this man. Payback which will be violent and could land your ass in jail, and you're telling me not to get upset." Tamara closes her eyes, pausing, drawing in a deep breath and holding up a finger. But when she opens her eyes again, there's nothing but fire there. "This coming from a man who lost his shit when I went to visit a friend in prison. I thought we were a team. There are certain things we do or don't do because of that team. I didn't hear you asking me if you could go."

I grab her finger which is still between us and push her hand down, trying to grab a hold of her. "Baby. Come on."

"Don't come on me." She wiggles free of me.

I laugh. "Don't come on you," I tease, loving how dirty it sounds and how I want nothing more than to come on her.

Her mouth flattens, and her eyes turn into tiny slits. "I'm dead fucking serious, Mammoth."

"Okay. Okay." I throw up my hands, surrendering to her. "He punched her in the face," I tell her, explaining where I'm coming from.

"What?" Her gaze moves to my mom and then back to me. "How can someone hurt Jessica? Can I come? Obviously, he needs a woman to teach him the lesson."

"Ma took a sledgehammer to him."

She rocks back again, dropping her arm from her hip. "No shit?"

"Yep."

"Fuck. That's some powerful shit."

"I know," I agree, reaching for her and finally getting a grip on her shoulders. "So, can I go? Do I have your permission?" I don't grit my teeth or flinch when I ask the question. Tamara needs to feel included in my decisions when the club isn't involved. I'm no longer just a me, but part of a we.

"You do. I'll stay with your ma."

"You can't stay here."

"Then neither can she," she argues, throwing that back at me quickly. "We can either both stay here, or she can come to our place or stay with someone else in the family. Uncle James and Thomas know how to hide people until she's clear from her trouble with the law."

"I don't want to get you or your family involved."

"I am involved. You are my family too, and they'd say the same. If your mom is staying here, so am I."

I grunt. "You're not staying here."

Tamara throws out her hands. "Look around, sparky. These are your friends. You know how they are. You really want to leave her here?" She shoots a look over my shoulder. "I mean, Morris is already looking pretty comfy with her."

I can't stop the growl from escaping my throat. "Fine. Take her back, but make sure she isn't staying at your place. The cops may look for her there."

"Someone in the family will take her. It's what we do."

I pull her close, sick of having space between us after being apart for too many days. "I love you, princess."

She touches my face, stroking my beard with her

thumb. "I love you too. Now—" she smiles "—I could use a drink."

"You just got here."

"Point?"

I nod, because I have nothing.

MAMMOTH'S KISS is slow and deliberate as he hovers above me. "I can't wait to have this every day," he murmurs against my lips, the hair on his legs rubbing against my inner thighs.

"We're another day closer, right?" I stare up into his gray eyes and force a smile on my face.

I know we're lying to each other. He'll never really be out. Not in the way we would hope or many would think. A brother is a brother for life. He knew that when he prospected. But he couldn't see beyond where he was, and that was alone.

The club rescued him during a time when he needed more. The military life had suited him, and once it was gone, he was lost. The Disciples have been good for him. They gave him purpose. They gave him family. They gave him a home. But now, there's no divorce or moving away without staying under their thumb.

"Sure, princess." Mammoth gives me a soft smile, resting his arms near my head, palms flat on the bed. "Another day closer."

"What's it going to be like?" I ask, pushing his hair back and holding it in my hands to see his face better. "Are you going to be on call?"

Mammoth laughs and then sobers. "Not quite like that, but I have to be available. And if—" he pauses, lowering himself enough to place his forehead against mine "—they start a club over by us, I have to be a member at least, if not the head."

My body stiffens, and I chew the inside of my lip to stop myself from saying something totally assholey.

"Don't worry about any of that right now. It's a long shot and just their way of letting me know the rules beforehand."

"Don't worry about it?" The asshole in me slips, and there's nothing I can do to stop it. "Morris and Tiny have us by the short hairs, and I'm just supposed to not worry about it?"

He moves his arms closer to my head before he holds my face in his palms. "Princess, I get where you're coming from. I know you're angry. But this is life. This is life with me. If you want out, now is the time to do it before I give everything up, sink a shit-ton of money into a business, and move across the state."

My stomach clenches. Is he saying what I think he's saying? I blink and push against his chest, trying to sit upright. "You want to break up?" I whisper.

He holds steady, keeping me under him, pushing me back down with his chest. "Did I say that?" he asks with his voice flat and low.

"Well, no." I sigh, relaxing back into the bed. "But it sure as hell sounded like that's where you were heading."

"I can't control what's out of my hands. I'm in the club. You knew this when we met. Knew this when we fucked. Knew this when you said you loved me."

I close my eyes, tears forming behind my eyelids. "I know. I just wish…"

"Fairy tales are for kids, Tam. We're adults. We have to deal with our shit instead of throwing a hissy fit every time something doesn't work out."

The sinking feeling in the pit of my stomach vanishes and is replaced by a deep, searing burn. "A hissy fit?" I narrow my eyes, pushing at his chest with more force until he finally backs away. "Is that what I'm having when I'm concerned about your safety and our future? Are you really saying this stupid shit to me?" I quickly crawl to the end of the bed, wanting to be standing for this.

He shifts, turning to sit on the edge of the bed, facing me. "Listen," he says, placing his hand on one leg, looking chill as fuck during a time when he shouldn't be.

I cross my arms over my chest, tilt my head, and ready myself. "I'm listening. This better be good."

"You can't lose your shit over everything. You just can't."

"I'm not losing my shit, and I can do whatever I want when it comes to us."

"Yes." He nods, running his fingers through his beautiful brown hair. "This is about *us.*" He throws his arm out toward me. "Not you. Not me. *Us.* But there's also the club. I've gone over this shit ad nauseum. I'm done with the conversation."

I step forward, turning my gaze down at him, seething. "You're done?"

"With the conversation," he growls. "I love you. I want a future with you. I'll put up with whatever club shit I need to in order for us to be happy and give you everything you want and need. I can't separate myself entirely. It's just the reality. You in, princess, or are you out?" His thumbs stroke the tender skin near my biceps, giving me goose bumps.

"In," I say without even thinking.

I've been stupid for the man since the moment I laid eyes on him. If I were smart, I would've run as far away from the Disciples as I could. If I weren't so hopelessly in love, I wouldn't have seen him again after the lockdown. But I can't close my heart to him. He's the only man I've ever really loved.

When I almost lost him to the shooting, I knew he was everything to me. I mean, I knew it before, but that moment, the hell he went through, solidified everything in my mind. There was no questioning if we were right for each other or if we should be together. I couldn't imagine a life without Mammoth.

"But…"

"There's always a but." He grunts, hardening his jaw.

I shrug, giving him a smile as I step closer to him. "But you need to be honest with me. I need to know things."

His gray eyes meet mine. "Like what things?"

"Well," I say, talking super sweet as I move his hand and climb into his lap, straddling his legs. "Everything. You know?"

"I don't know." He snakes his arm around my back, placing his hand on my ass. "There are things I can never tell you."

My hands find his shoulders as I settle in. "Like what?"

"Club things," he says.

"I know a lot more than you think," I tell him.

"You do?"

I nod.

"How?" He digs his fingers into my ass cheeks.

My belly does a funny flip as I slide forward and my pussy presses against his cock. "I don't know. I just do."

He raises an eyebrow. "You eavesdropping?"

I shrug. "Maybe."

"You tossing my phone?"

Damn. I don't want to admit it, but I've done it a few times. I felt such guilt afterward too. I never like my privacy invaded, but here I am, doing it to him. It is only when he is cagey about things. Which, in all reality, is a lot.

I mean, I get it. He has to be.

There are things in his life that are meant to stay inside the club. Girlfriends and old ladies aren't *in the know,* and I've tried to accept that fact and failed.

"Possibly," I whisper, holding back a laugh.

He tips his head forward, nuzzling against my neck. As his lips skate across my skin, I bend my body back, using it as a means to change the subject.

"Possibly?" he murmurs against my skin. "Will you have an orgasm again tonight? Possibly."

I bite my lip, laughing quietly. "You're being rude again."

"You can't toss my phone." Mammoth's mouth slides down my neck to my collarbone. "It's a hard line."

"You guys shouldn't be texting anyway. The government can read them too."

He pulls back and stares at me with nothing but fire in his eyes. "No more. You understand?"

"Yeah. Yeah. I understand," I tell him, but I'm at war with myself. I knew before that he wouldn't be happy, but I did it anyway. There are times when I just can't help or stop myself. "Just promise me you'll get better at communication."

"I'm great at communicating," he argues.

I roll my eyes. "You are not. You're great at communicating when we're fuckin' or you want to be fuckin'. But other times…"

The roughness of his palm scrapes against my skin as he adjusts my position. "I will try harder."

"Good," I tell him, smiling, trying to ignore the deep ache I feel between my legs again.

"We gotta go out there." He tips his head toward the door, and I sigh.

"I don't want to," I argue.

"Ma's here," he reminds me, and then he sighs. "Not exactly how I want to spend tonight, but it is what it is."

I unfold myself from his body and tiptoe across the room. "This was like old times."

Since Mammoth's mom is going to be staying in his room for the night, we've been downgraded to Pike's old room. It's been empty for years, and

Morris refuses to allow it to be filled by a new prospect. Now it's a place for wayward travelers or visitors.

"Old times?" he asks, watching me as I bend over and overtly show him my entire backside.

"Fuckin' in this old room."

"You mean good times," he says, climbing to his feet.

I'm unable to look away. His long, lean body covered in muscle shakes as he stretches. "The best," I whisper in reply, but I'm not only talking about the memories of our time in this room.

"Get that out of your head right now," he tells me, reading my mind.

"The night is young." I waggle my eyebrows. "We just have to put your ma to bed."

"The night is too young for that. Now, we have to spend the next few hours keeping the guys away from her. They're due back from a ride, and you know how they are about new women in the compound."

"They're hound dogs, but as soon as they find out she's your mom, they'll back off."

He laughs. "Really? You don't think a few would fuck her just to say they fucked my mother?"

"Stop," I tell him, covering my ears with my hands. "You're being ridiculous and gross."

He blinks at me, serious as a heart attack. "Tell me they won't." He throws up his arms, letting out a loud, frustrated grunt. "Morris is already sniffing around. You saw it with your own eyes."

"Morris is just being nice." I pull his old Mötley Crüe T-shirt over my head, which I stole from his closet the last time I stayed overnight. It's mine now. He's never getting the shirt back. It's super soft and big.

He shakes his head, eyeing the shirt, but doesn't say anything before he grabs his jeans. "You're too naïve."

"You think too much with your dick." I tick my chin toward his cock, which is waving around as he pulls up his jeans.

"Just like every man out there."

He has a point. I won't tell him he has that point, though, because I want to ease his tension, not feed into it. "They won't touch her," I promise him, although I can't technically deliver on it. "Plus, do you think your ma would do the nasty with any of them?"

Mammoth doesn't answer as he sits down on the edge of the bed and yanks on his boots. "I'm done talking about this."

"Okay," I mutter, laughing and getting a glare in return. "Seems to be the theme tonight."

We're talking about Jessica. The woman wouldn't know how to handle a biker in the sack if her life depended on it. Clearly, she's had sex before. She did have Mammoth after all, but that doesn't mean she's ready to get down and dirty now.

Mammoth stalks out of the room a moment later without another word. I toe on my sandals and run after him, plastering myself to his back as he walks into the main room of the compound. He stops as his boots hit the tile floor, and his gaze sweeps through the room, searching for her.

"Motherfucker," he whispers.

I peer around him, following his eyes. "What?" I ask, seeing nothing but a sea of bodies and a lot of skin.

"Look." He ticks his head toward the bar. "I fuckin' told you."

I grimace. "Well, at least they're not bangin'."

Shit.

His head snaps back and his eyes narrow. The gray is filled with so much fire, I can feel the burn. "At least they're not bangin'?"

I nod, smiling the most bullshit fake smile ever. "I'm not wrong."

"Christ," he mutters under his breath, grabbing my hand. "Let's go break that shit up."

"Oh, goodie," I whisper sarcastically.

This should be a fun time.

Mammoth pulls me forward, and my feet follow, keeping up with his large strides. He's determined. His eyes are laser focused on his mom and the way

Morris is leaning over her at the bar, arm propped up, looking like he's peeking down the cute scoop neck sundress I brought her.

Morris turns, eyes finding Mammoth and me, and backs away a foot. "Hey," he says casually, arm still resting on the bar as he tips his chin upward like his ass wasn't just busted.

"Hey," I say, drawing out the word.

Mammoth squeezes my fingers, and I know he wants me to shut up and not be nice to Morris, but… it's Morris. Then there's the fact that I don't really love being told what to do and I'm shit at following directions.

"Whatcha two doing?" I ask, being nosy and filling the silence as Jessica stares at Mammoth, and Mammoth stares at Morris. "Can we join you?" I twist my body a little, knowing full well I'm stirring a pot I shouldn't be stirring.

Jessica's eyes finally move away from Mammoth and meet mine. "Please," she says, pleading with her eyes as she says the words. "We were just talking about you." Those words, she says to Mammoth. When he doesn't respond but just stands there hard as granite, glaring at Morris, she says, "I'm talking to you. Are you listening to me, Jo…JD?"

Holy shit. She almost went there and used his real name. She almost outed him to the entire club, something he's never done in all the years he's been here. That would've added insult to injury, ratcheting up the tension even higher than the blistering level it is already at.

"I love your hair like that," I blurt out, because it's different from the last time I saw her when we video chatted, and I'm trying to defuse the situation and divert everyone's attention. "It's different, right?" I don't wait for her to respond and keep on going. "It looks different."

Another squeeze from Mammoth's hand and I bite my lip, stopping myself from continuing on the verbal shitting my mouth is doing.

"We'll sit," Mammoth grumbles, moving me in front of him like I'm a rag doll, and using my shoulder to push Morris to the side.

Well, okay. That wasn't overly aggressive or anything. I stand there for a moment, Morris almost pressed against me, wedged between him and Mammoth.

"Sorry," I whisper as a hand comes down on my shoulder, almost shoving me down in the seat.

Oh boy. I don't know who he thinks he's pushing around, but we're sure as fuck going to have words. I'll bite my tongue for a little bit, hopefully until we're in private, but if Mammoth doesn't get his shit together, it will happen right here in front of everyone.

"It's okay, kid," Morris says, taking a step back so

he's not in my space. His eyes are soft when he says it, being the sweet guy I sometimes see when we are alone. "Not your fault your guy is manhandling you."

Oh no, he didn't. He went there. He said those words, and although they are right, they are so, so wrong.

CHAPTER ELEVEN

MAMMOTH

"WHAT'S WITH THE FACE?" Ma asks, jabbing me in the ribs with her bony elbow. "And the attitude?"

Morris and Tamara are busy in a hushed conversation, ignoring my mother and me. I'm good with this. As long as she's keeping Morris busy, he's not trying to get in my mother's pants.

"Morris isn't someone I want you involved with."

Ma jerks her head back and blinks. "What?"

"You heard me," I mumble against the rim of the third beer I've had tonight. "Don't need to repeat it."

Her lips twist, and her blue eyes focus in on me, laser-sharp. It's the same look she used to give me as a little boy when she was trying to calm herself down so she didn't say something she'd regret later. "You think I'm going to date Morris?"

"Not date, Ma." I laugh. "Morris doesn't date."

"How would I get involved with him, then?"

My mother can't seriously be this clueless. She has to know Morris has been hitting on her. He isn't just being nice because she's my mother. The man does nothing unless there's an upside for him, and crawling between my mother's legs is surely that.

I raise an eyebrow, holding that bottle to my lips again, and don't reply. I wait, staring at her until I see the moment it clicks.

She gasps and smacks my arm, eyes brimming with anger. "I'm not that kind of woman, JD. How dare you say that?"

"He's that kind of man, Ma. Don't forget that shit. He'd eat you up and spit you out without a second thought."

Right now, standing next to the bar, I know the Morris of today way better than I know my mom. I knew the woman she was when I was younger. More than a decade of time passing has a way of changing a person. Sure, she hasn't gone all *"Girls Gone Wild,"* but maybe she is looking to take a walk on the biker side, spread her wings a little. The one thing I know— that shit is not happening with my brother and not at my club.

"Tomorrow, you're leaving," I tell her, giving her no room for an argument.

"And would you like to tell me where I'm going?"

She tilts her head, lips tight, blinking like there's something in her eyes. "Or are you going to order me around like I'm one of your women?"

I grunt, studying my mother's face, wondering what she knows about "my women." I've never shared my life with her. Kept her clueless because I was pretty sure her bible study never talked about what it meant to be dominated in the bedroom. "You want to explain that statement?"

Her eyes move to Tamara and then slice back to me. "You push that sweet girl around like she doesn't have a mind of her own. Maybe she didn't want to sit between Morris and me, but you literally shoved her onto the stool. No asking. No wondering where she wanted to plant her butt. You just put her there like she was another thing in your life you felt you could boss around."

"Seriously?" I jerk my head back, feeling the burning coil deep in my gut start to heat. "That's what you think of me?"

"I know all about you, son. I know more than you ever thought I knew. I pay attention. I may go to church, you may think I'm a prude, but I'm not blind. It doesn't matter what you do in your own bedroom—God knows I don't want to hear about it—but you cannot treat a woman that way." She reaches out and presses her finger into my chest. "I didn't raise you to treat *your* woman that way."

My eyes dip down to where our bodies are connected. "I treat Tamara like a queen, Ma. She's everything to me."

"Are you kidding me?"

"One hundred percent dead serious. Tamara is my world. She's everything to me. I do whatever I can to make her happy. I'm giving up the club for her, moving across the state for her."

"You shoved her on that stool like a rag doll."

Shit. I did do that. It wasn't my intention, but having my mother here, with the guys, has me more on edge than if someone were pointing a gun in my direction. I don't know why. It shouldn't matter. Ma is like Mother Teresa. I need to remind myself she's just being friendly and nothing more. But telling myself that and believing it are two different things.

I set my beer down and sit back, letting out a long breath. "I wasn't myself."

"I think you were very much yourself," she shoots back immediately, blue eyes narrowed. "You were always a bossy, cocky thing."

My hand moves to my neck, rubbing the tight skin, thinking about my next words very carefully. "I'm not being myself right now. I'm sorry, Ma. I don't normally push Tamara around. You have my head all twisted. Trust me, the woman is like a granite monument."

Ma tips her chin up, throwing massive attitude as she tells me, "A woman needs to be if she's with you."

I sigh. "I'll try to be a better man," I promise her.

Ma smiles sweetly and lifts her hand to my face. "Good, baby. None of us is perfect, but that doesn't mean we should stop trying to do better…be better."

"I'm doing that."

"So, are you going to tell me where I'm going tomorrow or dance around the subject?"

"I've got something to do." I grab my beer, keeping my eyes trained on my ma. "You're going home with Tamara for a few days until that something is done."

Her face, which had softened, hardens again. "I don't need to bother Tamara. I don't need a babysitter. The woman has a life and doesn't need this old lady in her space."

"She wants you to go with her," I tell her.

"Tam," Ma calls out, glancing over my shoulder to where Tamara and Morris are still shooting the shit, giving us time to talk.

"Yeah, Jess?" Tamara says into my back.

"You want me at your place?"

"Sure do, Jess. I'd love to show you around my town and for you to meet my family."

I can't stop the smirk from spreading across my face. If I were younger, Ma would've told me to wipe it off.

"Well…" Ma pauses, gaze moving to me, narrowing, and then going back to Tamara. "Okay."

"Do you not want to come home with me?" I can hear the sadness in Tamara's voice. She's putting on a show, though. She's playing on my mother's guilt and need to please. It's something she learned from her family. Any type of pushback is met with guilt and usually works. I know it will work on my mother, and so does Tamara.

"Don't be silly, sweetie. Of course I want to go home with you."

"Good," Tamara replies, swiveling around on her stool and wrapping her arms around my middle, plastering her chest to my back. "This is going to be the best time ever. You can tell me everything about JD when he was little."

"I have so many stories I can tell you," Ma teases, eyes dancing with humor as I groan. "He wasn't always this grumpy, big guy."

"He's not so bad. A little testy at times and bossy the other times." Tamara's warm breath skids across the skin of my neck as she speaks, and I turn my head, eyes meeting hers, and our mouths are so damn close, I could kiss her without moving much. "And yet, I love the big lug." Her eyes dance as she looks at me.

"You wouldn't love me if I weren't all those things, princess. Not to mention, I could describe you the same way. Plus, you'd destroy a weaker man."

Her eyebrows rise. "I'm never bossy."

I bark out a laugh. "You are *so* bossy."

"Am not."

"Are," I say, smiling as I soak in her beauty.

"Tamara is the sweetest woman you've ever been with," Ma replies, even though we're no longer talking to her.

"Bullshit," Morris coughs, earning him a glare from me.

"How many have you met?" Tamara asks, opening the can of worms my mom decided to throw on the bar.

"A few," she tells Tamara as I turn my body, giving my mother a hard and somewhat cautious stare.

"Ma, I was a teenager the last time you met a girl —and I mean, a girl."

She shrugs and moves her front toward the bar, reaching for her drink. "They still count."

"Was he into the cheerleaders or the band girls?" Tamara asks against my ear. "I need to know all the things."

"Oh, honey." Ma gives her a devilish smile. "I'll tell you all the things."

"No. No, you won't," I tell her, pointing my finger at my ma. "The past is in the past. Leave it there."

Tamara presses her tits against my back. "Don't worry, sparky. Your mom and I will have plenty of time to talk the next few days."

"Fucking fantastic," I mutter under my breath.

"We'll save the good stuff for when we're alone." Ma nods, smiling so damn big she's almost laughing. "I got you, boo."

Tamara chuckles. "There's something so wrong with those words coming out of your mouth, Jessica."

"Ma," Ma corrects her, almost knocking me backward.

"Ma?" Tamara asks.

"It's time, honey. We both know where this is going. Might as well get used to it now."

"Ma," Tamara repeats. "I like that."

In all honesty, I do too.

I don't care Ma is going to tell Tamara all about my ex-girlfriends and the weird phases I went through in high school. The only thing I care about is the fact that my ma is smiling and laughing after all the shit she went through. Whatever makes her happy and keeps her smiling, I am all for, even if it is at my expense.

"Jessica, you want a new drink?" Morris asks, making his way around the bar and planting himself right in front of my mother.

"I could use something a little more…" She trails off as he reaches underneath, but his face moves closer to hers.

Never gonna happen, man.

"Stiff or soft, sugar?" he asks her, and I growl.

Her eyes widen, and every muscle in my body stiffens at the sexual innuendo.

"Ma, you want liquor or pop?"

"Pop," Tamara snorts. "It's soda."

"I think I could go for some Johnnie Walker."

Morris blinks. "Sugar, we have scotch. Johnnie Walker is a bit beyond the club's budget."

"Whatever you have, Morris." Ma smiles, watching him as he moves, looking at him in a way I'm not liking much.

He pulls down the bottle from the shelf behind the bar, grabs a fresh glass, and pours her more than necessary. "Now, if you let me know the next time you're coming, I'll be sure to get some Johnnie for you."

Ma's smile grows, and her cheeks turn this shade of pink that's clear as day even in this shitty lighting.

"She's not coming back," I tell Morris, setting the record straight.

Ma turns her face slowly, glare firmly planted. "Zip it, kid," she tells me.

I jerk my head back, shocked at my ma's ability to still want to put me in my place, and the speed at which she did it.

"She told your ass," Tamara whispers in my ear.

Morris laughs, the small lines near his eyes deepening. It takes everything in me not to haul my ass over the bar and punch him in his goofy-faced grin.

"Don't listen to Mr. Crabby," she tells Morris, leaning forward, placing one elbow on the bar, and reaching for the glass he placed in front of her with her other hand. "He's protective. He never grew out of it."

"A man should always protect the women in his life," Morris replies, leaning forward too, like they're old chums.

Tamara squeezes my middle. "Relax. You're so fucking tense."

"How can I?" I whisper, keeping my eyes directed at the two flirting with each other, not giving a single shit I'm here.

"Because they're just talking and flirting. No harm. No foul."

I turn my face, meeting Tamara's gaze as I do. "No harm? No foul?"

She nods, splaying her hands across my stomach. "Do you honestly think Jessica would sleep with him?" she whispers in my ear.

"No." My answer is immediate. "First, because she just beat the shit out of her boyfriend, and second, because Morris isn't her type."

"Then calm the fuck down," she bites out and hardens her stare.

I stare back, blinking. "What?"

"What? What? You heard me."

I blink again. "I did hear you. Heard every short, sharp word, princess. Just surprised."

The music in the room shifts to "Wonderful Tonight" by Clapton, and Ma straightens her back. "Oh. My. God. I love this song so much."

"It's a good one." Morris nods, smiling.

"Dance with me. Will you, Morris?" she asks, giving no shits I'm sitting right next to her, pissed as hell about their flirtation.

Morris's eyes come to me for a second but then immediately go back to my mother. "Whatever makes you happy."

The burn deep in my gut grows into a raging inferno as he rounds the bar and holds out his hand to her.

"We don't really dance here…"

Tam squeezes me again with her silent *shut the fuck up*.

"There're no rules," Morris informs my ma as he pulls her away from the stool, ignoring me.

"Let her have some fun. She's been through enough without your bullshit on top of it," Tamara tells me as my mother stands, her hand in Morris's.

I stare at my ma, watching as she moves toward the middle of the floor. My body tightens as Morris wraps an arm around her back, and she curls into him, head on his shoulder.

"She needs this. She needs the comfort right now."

"I can comfort her," I tell Tamara, watching Morris's hands and the way he holds my mother carefully.

"It's not the same. You're her kid. She needs to feel the safety of a man who isn't her blood wrapped around her."

I grunt, hating every second of the way they're moving to the sweet words being sung.

"You don't have to like it, baby. But for the love of God, give her tonight to feel at peace."

My face softens with her words. Ma has been through enough. Probably more than I even realize, seeing as she took a sledgehammer to a man's body. Something I never thought she'd have in her, no matter what anyone did to her.

Clearly, I was wrong.

Tomorrow, I'll take care of him.

But tonight, I'll let her take care of herself.

I TIP MY HEAD BACK, soaking in the sunshine as I stand outside the compound, waiting for Mammoth's mom. "I wish you weren't going out of town, but coming home with us instead."

Mammoth slides his arms around my waist and pulls me closer until he blocks out the sun. "I'll be at your place tomorrow. We don't plan on sticking around."

"Promise me you'll be careful," I whisper as I stare across the field, no longer feeling the warmth of the sun but the heat of his body. "You're still not healed."

"I promise," he says softly.

"Promise me you'll come back."

"I promise that too."

I relax against him, loving the way his arms feel

wrapped around me and the hardness of his chest. He grunts as the door opens and his mom saunters out wearing the most adorable pink sundress with white flowers. Morris is right behind her, hands to himself, not crowding her personal space.

"You take care of yourself, yeah?" Morris says to Jessica as Mammoth and I shift our bodies in their direction.

"I will, Morris. And if anyone gives me shit, I still have my sledgehammer."

Morris laughs, his teeth sparkling in the bright sunshine. "You're one of a kind, Jessica. Come back sometime and visit."

"Over my dead body," Mammoth whispers, earning him a smack to his good arm.

They're cute together. Jessica's older than Morris by a little over a decade, and Morris has never been one to go for older chicks, but they'd make an awesome couple.

"Stop thinking it," Mammoth grumbles.

"What?"

"They're not getting together."

Busted. How does he do that?

"I wasn't thinking that," I lie, wondering how I'm so damn transparent and the man can almost always read my mind.

"Liar," he teases playfully.

"Sugar, you don't need a sledgehammer when you

have your son and me. Anyone gives you shit, and I mean anyone, you call either of us and it'll end."

Jessica's smile grows wider as she throws her arms around Morris's wide shoulders. "You're the best."

He's hesitant at first, not sure what to do with the woman who's wrapped around him like he's a savior. "It's nothing." Slowly, he snakes his arm around her back, keeping the hug as PG as a hug normally is. "It's what family does for one another, and we're family." Morris's arm falls away, and Jessica takes a step back, still smiling.

"Thank you again," she tells him, brushing her brown hair off her shoulders as the wind kicks up, trying to take her hair along with the hem of her dress. "I should really just turn myself in and save you guys the trouble."

Mammoth starts to move, but I tighten my grip on the arm he has wrapped around my body. "Don't," I whisper, and he actually listens.

Morris reaches out, placing his hands on her shoulders. "Your son and I will get this fixed. You will not turn yourself in. Get that thought right out of your head. We will make sure you're safe and never have to worry about that asshole again. This is our job, our duty."

Jessica gawks at Morris. "Your job and your duty?"

He nods back in response.

"How is it your job and duty?" Then she peers over her shoulder in our direction. "Or his? I'm the parent here. I'm the oldest. It's my job and duty to shelter him from the storm and keep him safe. I spent most of my life doing those things. At no point do those roles reverse. I may be a woman and, yes, I may be older, but I can handle things on my own. That may come as a shock to some, especially to the man sitting in Georgia with his arm all busted because I decided I'd had enough and grabbed that heavy hammer from the garage, taking it to his body like I was playing Whack-a-Mole."

Morris's smile is soft. "Sugar," he says, drawing out the word and speaking softly.

I like it every time that word rolls off his tongue even if it's pointed at Jessica.

"Around here, we take care of one another. Doesn't matter who's who. If someone is hurting someone we love, we deal with it together. No one is on their own, especially not our women."

"I'm not one of your women," she argues.

Morris's eyes move to us. "You're his mom. Therefore, you're one of ours."

Jessica shakes her head.

"Zip it," Morris tells her, throwing her words from last night back at her. "Nothing you say or do will change that. All the arguing in the world won't make it any different. Maybe you don't know how true family works, but this is how our family works. You are not alone. You don't have to go fighting every battle without backup. And since you've been wronged, we're going to make it right."

"Ma," Mammoth calls out, yelling right in my ear. "Come on. It's getting late, and we already have a ride ahead of us."

She peers over her shoulder, Morris's hands still on her. "Can I take my car?"

Mammoth shakes his head. "Hell no. There's a warrant out for you, and you don't know the area like Tamara. She'll drive you, and the guys will store the car out of view."

"But…"

"No buts, Jessica." Morris squeezes her shoulders, and she turns her eyes back to him. "We'll hold your car, and when shit is clear, you'll get it back. No more lip. No more talking. Just get that ass moving so we can get ours riding."

I chuckle, liking the way Morris is handling her, even though he is, in fact, handling her. I've never liked when men try to push women around, but right now, her mind is fuzzy, and she isn't thinking right.

Morris is. He's always steps ahead, planning his next move before the other person has even had a chance to figure out how they feel about the last move.

"What a clusterfu—"

"Shh," I tell Mammoth, leaning back into him, making him take my weight. "She's not going to listen to anyone except him."

Mammoth laughs softly, his body shaking against mine. "Ma listens to no one, and she won't listen to him."

"She will."

"Nope."

"Yep. She'll eventually get it. I didn't want to listen to you, but here I am."

Mammoth's laugh is louder. "You still don't listen."

"I'm a Gallo. I don't have the genetics. My blood makes me question everything, especially authority."

"You sayin' I'm the boss?"

I turn and press my palm to his beard. "Sparky, we both know you're bossy as fuck. But *the* boss?" I pause, smiling as his eyes narrow. "Only in the bedroom."

He stares at me for a few seconds, not saying a word, eyes hawkish. I swallow, waiting for him to shoot off at the mouth because he's Mammoth and sometimes we argue.

"Princess," he says, his voice smooth and deep. "You're cute."

I stare back at him and narrow my eyes this time. "I may be cute, but that doesn't mean I'm weak."

He moves his hands to my hips as his fingers dig

into the skin near the waistband of my shorts. "Weak women are boring. I love you for your strength with a side of wild."

"Just a side of wild?" I raise an eyebrow.

The corner of his mouth tips upward. "Thanksgiving-size side of wild."

I laugh, placing my hand on his chest. "You're ridiculous sometimes."

"Listen." The smile falls from his face, and the serious guy is back. "Head straight home. No stopping for even the smallest thing until you have my mom somewhere safe. Maybe next door at Pike's. If the cops are looking for her and know about you, they could show up at your place."

"I won't stop anywhere," I promise. "I'll stay on the backroads and off the highway."

"And Pike's, got it?"

"What about Aunt Izzy's or Lily's? Pike's place is so…so manly and small. She won't be comfortable there."

Manly is code for not very clean or very nice. The place is comfortable, and the furniture is broken in, but there's no extra room for another human unless they're going to sleep with one of the boys.

"Whatever you think is best. I trust you." He pulls me forward by the hips and bends his neck. "Now, give me that mouth before you go."

My belly does this little flip as his eyes drop to my lips. "You want a kiss?"

"Stop fuckin' with me, Tam. We're on a schedule, and we're already behind. I want that mouth, and I need it now before you have to go."

"Bossy," I whisper, lifting my face to his.

"You love it," he says back as he moves his lips toward mine.

"I love you," I reply. "Not your attitude."

"Ditto, princess. Ditto." But before I can say another word, his mouth is on mine, pressing hard. His kiss is forceful and demanding, wanting tongue in front of our audience of two. One of whom is his mother and not someone I want to tongue-kiss my guy in front of.

I hold back, and Mammoth feels it, digging his fingers into my skin and kissing me hard.

"Ready?" his mom asks from our side.

I pull away like we're in high school and I was just caught on my knees giving him a blow job.

"Yeah. We should, um, go," I mumble, suddenly embarrassed.

"Ma, you're killing me here."

"You look very much alive, JD," Jessica shoots back.

I chuckle, loving the way she handles him and is able to stop him dead in his tracks. "We better go. We have a long drive."

"Text me when you're back and safe," he tells me.

"You do the same," I tell him, snaking my arms around his middle and hugging him tight.

Mammoth presses his lips to my hair, smelling me. "I will, princess. I love you," he whispers.

I tip my head back, looking into his gray eyes. "I love you too."

He kisses me again, this time softly before pulling away. A small pat on the ass is my signal we're officially done and it's time for us to get moving. "We'll follow you out."

I nod and release my hold on him, wishing this weren't goodbye. "Okay," I whisper, holding back the tears I know are forming as my vision starts to blur.

"No crying, princess. This isn't goodbye. I'll see you tomorrow."

I nod again, biting my lip.

"Ready?" Jessica asks, touching my shoulder.

I turn as I pull down my sunglasses from the top of my head, hiding my emotion from everyone else except Mammoth. "Always. Let's get you somewhere safe and more to your liking."

Jessica laughs and shakes her head. "It's not so bad here."

I jerk my head back, and my mouth drops open. "Not so bad?"

She nods as she rounds the hood of my car with

Mammoth and Morris heading toward the truck. "I thought it would be worse, honestly."

I stare at her across the roof as I reach for the handle. "Worse, how? I mean, it's not awful, but it's not the Ritz or even a roadside motel."

She opens the door, sliding into the seat, and I do the same. "I know you think I'm some old-school prude, sitting at home reading my bible and knitting blankets for my future grandkids."

"I do not," I blurt out, but she called me on my shit. That's exactly how I've pictured her every time Mammoth has talked to her when I've been around. Maybe not the knitting part, but I knew church was a big part of her life. I could never picture her inside a biker compound and most definitely never imagined her saying it wasn't bad.

"You're a shit liar, Tamara." Jessica chuckles as she fastens her seat belt and settles in. "I get it. I do. I'm not as wild as you. I used to be when I was younger. I used to have a carefree attitude until life made me face the stark realities of the fragility of our time here. After Mammoth's daddy died, I had a moment when I was reckless, but then I had a kid to raise alone and my butt snapped back to my responsibilities pretty damn quick."

"Yeah," I whisper, turning the key in the ignition and watching Mammoth settle into the passenger side of his pickup truck with Morris at the wheel. "I'm sure that makes you tame the inner wild pretty damn fast."

She nods.

"I'm not judging you," I tell her, easing the car out of the parking spot and preparing to hit the road. "Please don't ever think that."

"Never thought you were, sweetheart." She smiles as she studies me from the passenger seat, fidgeting with the bottom of her sundress. "I just want you to know I'm not a judgmental person. Life's too short to worry about what other people are doing. You need to do you and make sure you have that inner peace. The world's going to hurl enough bad shit your way. You don't need to pile on top of it with your own bad juju."

"Okay," I whisper, listening to every word she's saying, getting deeper with me than she ever has before.

"Just like that asshole. He gave me enough bad until I decided to take that business into my own hands. Him, I judge because he got physical with me. But those guys—" she glances toward the clubhouse "—they're living their best life."

I nod. "I can't argue that. Maybe not their best life, but the one that makes them happy."

"Happiness is the most important thing in life. Too damn short to be miserable."

"That's the truth," I whisper as Morris and Mammoth pull up behind us. "Guys are ready."

Jessica motions toward the driveway. "Well, do you want me to stop talking, or do you like my chatter?"

I pull forward, the guys moving behind us. "It's a long drive, Jess. Talk all you want. It'll help the time go faster. Why don't you tell me more about Mammoth as a little kid? I know how he is now, which is sometimes a complete pain in the ass, but I don't know much about when he was little. He doesn't open up often."

And by often, I mean never.

He's given me the overview, telling me the critical points, but not a full picture. A boy doesn't lose his daddy and not feel the deep burn of that loss in his soul. Mammoth has become good at hiding the pain, but I know it's there, bubbling under the surface.

"Josiah was a sweet boy. Always content. Always laughing."

"Always laughing?" I shrug. "Hard to picture him a giggly little thing. He's just so…so…"

"Big and grumpy?" She finishes my statement for me.

"Kind of," I mutter, holding back my laughter.

"He wasn't always like that. He was sweet and bubbly, but the older he got…" She shakes her head, turning her face toward the window, no doubt hiding whatever emotion is passing through her eyes.

"I can't imagine not having my dad. We're inseparable."

"Most girls find first love in their father and learn how they should be loved."

I roll to a stop at the gates, waiting for them to open, and I slide my eyes to the rearview mirror, soaking in Mammoth and hoping it's not the last time I see him breathing.

I never worried like this before. Never gave our time a second thought. I never worried he'd get shot or end up in the ground. But now, since he was shot, it's the only thing on my mind.

"Gate's open," Jessica tells me, because I'm so wrapped up in gawking at Mammoth, I hadn't even noticed.

"Sorry," I mutter, easing my foot off the brake and finally heading out of the compound. "I was just…"

"Staring at my boy?" she asks point-blank.

I chuckle. "Well, yeah. He's just so…"

She reaches over and pats my arm. "I know he's a looker. Always has been. He's always been eye-catching and had a way with the ladies."

"That's one way to describe him," I mumble, feeling the nasty ball of jealousy in my stomach.

"He's completely in love with you though, Tamara. I've never seen him look at someone the way he looks at you. So, wipe that look right off your face."

I glance her direction only for a moment, shocked. "What look?"

"Jealousy."

"I'm not jealous. I've never been the jealous type," I say defensively, sounding every bit jealous and petty.

"Mm-hmm," she murmurs. "Whatever you need to tell yourself, baby. But when a woman's in love, really in love, and as smitten as you are, sometimes the little green monster rears its ugly head. I saw what was happening in the clubhouse. I also saw how the women were dressed. I should say, how little they were wearing. It's only natural that you're a little jealous and protective of the man you love."

"He'd never cheat," I say quickly, gripping the steering wheel so tight, my knuckles start to pale.

"But that doesn't mean it'll stop those bimbos from trying to get with him. Women are ruthless, especially those kinds of women. They flaunt what they have, trying to tempt men with their skimpy clothes. But don't worry…my son is too smart for that."

I sigh. "I know, Jessica. I know."

"Good," she says and leans forward, looking at something in the distance. "Is that a red pickup?"

I squint, trying to see the color with the sunlight

shining in my eyes. "I think so. There's a man next to it too, I think."

"Stop the car!" she screeches, grabbing the dashboard. "Stop the goddamn car."

I slam my foot on the brake as my eyes move to the rearview mirror, and the guys barely miss my bumper. "Fuck," I hiss as my hands begin to shake. "What's wrong?"

"It's him."

"Him who?"

"Sledgehammer," she whispers.

Oh fuck.

"WHAT THE HELL?" I ask Tamara as she and my mother get out of her car, eyes fixated on something or someone straight ahead.

What in the actual fuck are they doing? My orders were clear. Get in the car, head home, and do not stop for any reason.

Tamara tilts her head in the direction of the pickup in the distance. "It's him."

My mother stands behind the door, frozen. "He came for me," she says, her voice almost robotic. "Shit. How did he even find me?"

I narrow my eyes, seeing the white cast on the entire length of his arm. "Go back to the compound," I bark out as my body tightens and a burning knot forms in my stomach. "Tell Eagle, Ginger, and Tiny to get their asses out here."

This crazy turn of events is in our favor. I don't have to sit my ass in my pickup truck for hours, travel out of state, and take care of things. He's come to our turf, without backup, looking for trouble. Now, this isn't only about retribution, but protection. I'll make sure this piece of shit will never lay his hands on another woman again.

Tamara nods, but there's fear in her eyes. "Jessica, get back in the car," she tells my mother, waving at her. "Come on."

"Oh God. I knew I shouldn't have come here," Ma says, still not moving her ass. "I should've turned myself in."

"Ma!" I stalk toward her, done with her stalling. "Get your ass in the car, and get gone."

Ma turns her head, eyes wide, face tight. "Call the police," she whispers.

I keep my gaze trained on the man in the distance, leaning against the hood of his pickup as he watches us. "We are the law around here. Now, go. Listen to Tamara."

Ma blinks, processing my words, but her feet are still glued to the bit of cinder she's standing on. "I can talk him down."

"Like you did all the times he beat you?" I say, not thinking about how my words will impact her.

She flinches, feeling and hearing what I just said. "I'm going. Don't…"

I hold up a hand. "Just get in the fucking car and go!"

Finally, her feet come unstuck, and she folds her body back into Tam's car, as does Tamara. Morris and I glare straight ahead, keeping our eyes fixed on the guy as Tam turns the car around in the grass and leaves us in a cloud of dust.

"Ready for this?" Morris asks, coming to stand next to me.

"Never been more ready," I snarl.

Morris and I move forward, taking in the unarmed man with nothing more than his cast as protection.

If he's carrying, it's not visible. If he has a gun, I'm not sure how he'd shoot if he's right-handed since my ma decided to decimate his arm into a million little pieces, leaving him casted from wrist to shoulder.

"Where'd the bitch go?" he asks, pulling a toothpick from between his lips with his one good hand.

He's exactly my mother's type. Tall and lanky, hair cropped short like he wasn't able to let go of the style after leaving the military, clean-shaven, and wearing camo.

"The bitch?" Morris growls, cracking his knuckles as he walks next to me. "I know you didn't just call her a bitch."

The man smiles. "She's a woman, yeah?

Therefore, she's a bitch. A traitorous bitch, at that. She busted up my arm and needs to pay. She's my woman. My bitch. This ain't no business of yours." His eyes swing to me. "Or yours."

I let out a bitter laugh. "My ma is my business. She's not your business. You had your time with her. You did her wrong and she did you right, but she made one mistake."

"Ah. Josiah," he whispers, eyes squinting as he studies me, tossing the used toothpick to the ground. "Should've known she'd run to you without having to look at the GPS."

I draw my eyebrows inward, confused.

"Can't take a man's car with GPS on board and stay gone for long."

Fuck. Technology is sometimes a blessing, but other times…dangerous as hell. I didn't even think to ask her about her car or the possibility she could be tracked by the asshole. I was too worried about the cops showing up at the compound. I didn't think a man who would beat a woman would have the balls to show up here.

My fingers curl closed as I stalk toward the man, ready to wipe the smug grin off his face. Morris is right next to me, keeping step with me, just as ready to beat his ass.

"We puttin' him in the ground?" Morris asks quietly as we advance.

"Nah, man. Break his other arm," I mutter, knowing there're other ways to make a man pay.

The dick takes a step forward, putting his hands up, like that's going to save him. "I'm unarmed."

"And?" I growl.

He scurries toward the driver's door, reaching for the handle as Morris and I run up behind him. I grab him by the collar, hauling his ass backward.

"You shouldn't have come here, and now you're going to pay," I tell him, turning him around before throwing him back into the truck.

He flinches and cowers. "Please," he begs.

"Let me do this," Morris tells me, touching my shoulder as I reach back, ready to punch the guy. "I really want to do this."

"I'm going to teach him what it feels like to get punched in the face."

Morris backs away, throwing up his hands.

"Please, let me go. I won't say anything," the asshole pleads, holding his good hand up in front of his face like that's somehow going to protect him. "Please."

"Did my mother beg you for mercy when you hit her?" I snarl, and before he has a chance to answer, I throw the first punch, feeling the crunch of his bones against my knuckles.

"Now what?" Tamara asks, placing ice on my knuckles, insisting I need to do this, but I've never done it before. She's like a mother hen sometimes. No one has looked after me the way she does since I was a little kid. "What is Jessica supposed to do?"

"We're going to take her to your place and talk with James and Thomas."

"We're going to take her?" She raises an eyebrow, staring at me and no longer making faces at my bloodied hands.

I nod, wincing as she presses harder than necessary because she's too busy gawking at me. "I need to talk to them myself. I have to get her name cleared so she's not on the run forever."

"I can talk to them."

"Do you not want me to come?"

"Of course I want you to come, but don't you have to pack your things?"

"I threw the important shit in a duffel, and the rest the guys can pick over."

Eagle stalks into the clubhouse, running his fingers back and forth against his hair. "This is some bullshit. You should've put that man in the ground."

The guys are pissed. They wanted blood. They craved retribution for a woman they barely knew, because she gave birth to me. Although I want the man dead, now isn't the time. With a warrant out for my mother, and the electronic tracks he no doubt left, if he went missing and anyone realized it, all roads would lead back to her or us.

"He has two broken arms now. It's not enough punishment, but it's a start," I tell him as Morris walks in behind Eagle, whistling a cheerful, awkward tune. "What'd you do?"

"Me?" Morris presses his hand to his chest, looking innocent. "I don't know what you're talking about."

"Why are you so happy?" I ask, lifting Tamara's hand away from mine, giving her a small wink.

"Called a buddy of mine at the sheriff's. He picked up the asshole and was just going to hold him for twenty-four hours, but…" Morris laughs.

"What?" I ask.

"Dipshit has a warrant."

A smile immediately covers my face. "Nice," I mutter.

"It's a doozy too. He is going to be locked up for a long, long time."

"Huh." I laugh too, picturing him with two broken arms, trying not to become someone's bitch. "Didn't see that coming."

Morris fishes four beers out of the fridge, placing one each in front of Tamara, Eagle, and me, and keeping one for himself. "He had an attempted murder charge hanging over his head from Florida. He won't get any bail because he's a runner, and if we're lucky, he'll get the longest sentence allowable. Jessica shouldn't have to worry about him anytime soon."

I tip my bottle to him. "Nice work."

"Well, it's a damn good thing we didn't kill him," Eagle adds, which gets Tamara's attention and has her head turning so damn fast.

"Would you have?" she whispers against the rim of her beer.

"Never," he tells her, glancing at me for only a second. "We'd never do anything like that, doll. We're civilized human beings."

Tamara lets out a nervous laugh. "Of course," she whispers and keeps her eyes on Eagle as she tips the bottle back, chugging the cold beer.

"Jessica," Morris announces as soon as my mom walks into the main room from the hallway. "We're celebrating."

"Celebrating?" she asks, slowing her steps, peering around at the four of us.

"Yeah, sugar," Morris answers before I have a chance to, always inserting himself when my mother is involved. "Come have a drink."

I curl my empty hand, and Tamara touches my arm with her cold fingers. "Stop overreacting. He's not hitting on her."

"You sure?" I ask, raising an eyebrow, knowing Morris just as well as I know myself.

Ma slides onto a stool next to me and stares at Morris, blinking. "What happened? Did you…"

He shakes his head as he grabs another beer from under the bar. "Called the sheriff. The guy has a warrant. He won't be a problem for you."

Her eyes widen. "He won't?"

"Nope," Morris clips out, placing the bottle in front of her with a thud. "He's going to be someone's bitch for a long time. So, drink up, relax, and breathe a little."

Ma blots at her eyes as they tear up. "I need a minute," she says, before bolting from her stool toward the bedrooms.

"Dude," I say when she's out of earshot. I need him to know and set him straight. What he's been doing is not okay with me. "Why are you always hitting on my mom?"

Morris sets down his beer and leans forward, bringing his face close to mine. "I'm not hitting on her, Mammoth. Why the hell would you think that?"

Eagle shrugs next to him. "Sure as fuck feels like it."

"Jessica is your mom, yeah?" Morris asks me.

I nod.

"She's not a bitch or trash, right?"

I nod again.

"She came here in distress. Am I correct?"

I nod for the third time.

"Your woman is here too, so your hands are already full." He raises an eyebrow, turning his gaze toward Tamara. "Am I wrong?"

"No," I reply.

"I was just being nice. She's your mom. She's a woman in need who just went through a trauma. A woman doesn't do what she did without having some darkness in her. I wanted to give her something light. A little piece of sweetness she hasn't felt in a long time."

I sit here, staring at him in silence, taking in what he just said.

"Did I ever tell you about my mother?"

I shake my head as everyone else sits quietly, listening as closely as I am, but probably holding their breath. Tamara and Eagle both knew how I felt about the way Morris has been flirting with my mother. They knew there would be a moment when I'd finally had enough and would question him. The time is now, but instead of hearing what I thought, Morris is going to share about his personal life. About his past. Something he doesn't do often.

"My father was a miserable bastard. He took all that misery out on me every single day of my life. I was too little to do anything about it for years, but then, I grew the fuck up and I manned up. I learned how to get his attention and divert all his anger toward me instead of her. I took every punch, kick, or slap she would've for the last five years of her life." He closes his eyes, and when he opens them again, he stares at the bottle in front of him instead of me. "I was twelve when she was diagnosed with breast cancer. The woman never knew a day's peace. She never knew happiness. She never knew she was being loved wrong. The only thing that saved her from my miserable bastard of a father was death."

"I'm sorry, brother," I say, my voice tight and thick. "She didn't deserve that."

"She was the best of the best." He tips his head toward the hallway where Ma had disappeared. "Just like your mom. All sweet without an ounce of bad in her. I couldn't give peace to my mom, but I could make sure yours got it," he sighs, running his hand down his face. "I was just being nice, man. A woman like her needs someone to be nice, especially a man, so she doesn't forget we're not all like that jagoff who felt it was right and necessary to lay his hands on her. She needs to know she's worth more. Flirting? Nah, brother. I was just being thoughtful."

"Got it," I whisper, feeling like a fool.

Tamara elbows me in the ribs. "See, you big dummy?"

"Also, she's not my type, and even if she were, she's your mom, man. How much of an asshole do you think I am?"

"A pretty fuckin' big one," I tell him, laughing as I lift the beer to my lips again.

"She's welcome here anytime, but I don't think it's her type of place. Just make sure she finds that happy. Even if my mom never found hers, it would be nice to know someone else's did."

"I'll make sure she finds it," I tell him, and I mean every damn word.

CHAPTER
FOURTEEN

TAMARA

"THIS ISN'T how I wanted our first in-person meeting to go," Jessica tells me, sitting on my couch, shoulders slumped forward. "I wanted our first time seeing each other to be happy and fun."

"Well—" I scoot forward in my chair, resting my arms against my legs, exhausted "—today has been interesting, but don't feel bad about anything. Maybe when everything is all said and done, we can get a do-over."

"A do-over?" she asks, eyebrows furrowed and the small wrinkles near her eyes deepening.

"Yeah. We'll pretend this never happened. It's not a big deal."

I've done things where all I wanted was a do-over, and I'll be more than happy to give one to Jessica. She didn't do anything many women I know wouldn't do in her shoes. Everyone has a breaking point, and once she reached hers, she took matters into her own hands. I have to give the woman mad props for that.

"I wish it were that easy," she whispers.

"Everything will be fine. My uncles will be here in a few minutes, and we'll get everything sorted out."

She covers her face with her hands, shaking her head back and forth. "I can't believe this is how I'm meeting your family. How embarrassing."

I move across my small living room and take a seat next to her, sliding my arm across her shoulders. "Ma," I say, calling her the name she asked me to, but it sounds so foreign, I pause for a second. Her hands fall away from her face as she turns to me. "My uncles have dealt with stuff like this before. They're good guys. They're also guys who don't put up with men who place their hands on a woman. They won't judge you for what you did. They would've been there to help just like your son if they knew. You need to stop apologizing or worrying about what anyone else thinks of you. You protected yourself. You got away. There're plenty of women who cared too much about what others thought and aren't breathing anymore because of it. This is a no-judgment family when it comes to self-defense and doing what's right, and there's no doubt, you did what was right."

She curls over, hugging her knees. "The right thing to do would've been to call the cops."

I laugh. "He was a cop, and he's on the city council. They definitely would've taken his side and not yours, unless you called them as soon as he hit you with the evidence written all over your face."

"I didn't want anyone to see me like that."

"No one ever does." I rub her back, feeling the need to soothe her any way I can. "Society sometimes makes us feel like somehow we're to blame when we're the victims. When my uncles get here, you'll understand and feel better."

"I'm not sure I can ever feel better about what I did. I should've turned myself in and paid the price for my actions."

"And would he have paid the price for what he did to you?" I ask, shifting and tucking my leg under my body to face her. "He didn't look too bothered by the fact that he'd hit you or that you'd hit him, when he was outside the compound earlier."

The front door swings open, and Mammoth walks in, followed by Uncle Thomas and Uncle James. They look like a troublemaking trio ready to do some damage.

Mammoth's gaze swings from his mother to me, and I shrug with a grimace. I did my best to make her feel better after she cried most of the drive here once we left the compound.

"Ma," Mammoth says, kneeling in front of his

mother and placing her hands in his. "These are Tamara's uncles."

Jessica lifts her head, wiping her face near her eyes as she peers toward the door, soaking in the two giant men standing near the doorway. "It's nice to meet you," she says with a forced smile. "I'm so sorry you were dragged into this."

My uncles stalk into the living room, making the small space feel even smaller. Thomas takes a seat in the chair I just vacated, and James sits down on the coffee table in front of me.

He gives me a wink, and I smile, always loving my uncles and their crazy, badass vibes. There isn't a man in my family who isn't insanely protective, and I am blessed to have been born into this group instead of another. "Ms. Saint," James says, speaking softly and carefully. "I'm James Caldo, and behind me is my partner and brother-in-law, Thomas Gallo. We're Tamara's uncles. We're going to get you out of this."

She blinks, gawking at the two men, possibly intimidated by their size and the severity of their faces. They always look pissed off, especially when it comes to how women are treated, when they're in work mode. "Maybe I should turn myself in," she says for the hundredth time since she landed at the compound.

Mammoth squeezes her hands. "You will not," he tells her.

"No, ma'am," James adds. "There's no need to do that. In a small town such as yours, you wouldn't get a fair trial anyway. Thomas and I have no doubt we can get the charges dropped and have your name cleared pretty damn fast. We just need you to lay low, hold tight, and not do anything crazy like hand yourself over to the authorities."

Jessica takes one of her hands out of Mammoth's grip and reaches for the zipper of her purse. "Please let me pay you for your trouble."

Uncle James reaches out, placing his hand on her arm. "No, ma'am. We don't charge family, and even if you weren't family, we'd never let something like money get in the way of doing what's right, especially when it comes to domestic abuse."

Tears begin to stream down Jessica's face as she stares at my uncle, easing back into an upright position. "You're too kind," she whispers.

"Your son has filled us in on everything, and we already have our team assembling the necessary players. We need twenty-four to forty-eight hours to get this behind you, but we will, in fact, have you cleared."

I can't keep the stupid smile from my face. How did I get so lucky? Not only do I have two amazing and loving parents, but I am also fortunate enough to be surrounded by these men as uncles and even better women who taught me my self-worth and how to take care of myself from an early age.

"We've arranged for you to stay out of sight until everything has been settled. We're going to drop you off at our niece's house, where your ex will not find you, nor will the police," Uncle Thomas says, finally speaking from behind James. "They're more than happy to give you a comfortable place to stay and keep you safe as long as needed."

"Lily's?" I ask Uncle Thomas, to which I get a quick nod.

He scoots forward, reaching into his back pocket and fishing out a small flip phone. "Here's a burner phone. I'll need your cell phone so you're not tracked, but I'll return it once everything is settled."

"There's my phone," she says, moving her chin toward the small chunk of metal next to James on the coffee table. "I turned it off already."

"Most likely, they aren't tracking you. Resources are limited, and in the grand scheme of crimes and criminals, you're a small fish in a very big pond. But we'll take every precaution to make sure you stay missing for a few more days." James reaches forward and places the flip phone down before grabbing her phone. "The guys at the compound already removed your car's GPS and have stowed it away and out of sight. We're going to do everything in our power to keep you hidden, and all we ask in return is for you to stay put and not do anything to draw attention to yourself. Can you do that?"

She nods slowly. "I'll do whatever you tell me to, sir."

"Good," James replies, standing. "Thomas and I will take you to Lily and Jett's house on our way home. Hopefully by tomorrow night, this will all be a bad memory."

I stand too, finding myself wrapping my arms around my uncle's middle. "Thanks, Uncle."

He does the same, kissing the top of my head. "I love you, kid," he says, making me feel like a little girl again.

"Luckiest girl ever," I whisper as I smash my face into his chest, giving him one final squeeze.

"I'm feeling a little left out and slighted here, Tam," Uncle Thomas says, standing on the other side of the coffee table.

I laugh as I pull away from Uncle James, and he rolls his eyes. "He's always a whiny baby," Uncle James mutters.

My ass is around the table, hugging Uncle Thomas, a second later. "You're the best uncle a girl could ask for," I tell him, heaping praise on him too.

For as badass as Gallo men are, they do need their egos stroked every once in a while, just like every man on the planet. I learned that from an early age, my mother and aunts filling me in on the realities of male fragility and ego.

"You about done?" James asks Thomas as he gives me a last giant hug, making my feet come off the floor. "We got important shit to do, brother."

"Ma, I'll walk you out and grab your bag out of Tamara's car."

"Okay," Jessica whispers. "Whatever you want, honey."

"Don't worry. Promise me you won't worry or do something foolish?" he asks his mom, holding her by the shoulders and peering down at her.

"I won't do anything foolish."

He smiles. "Good. Lily is the sweetest human being I've ever met. You're a lot like her, and I have no doubt she'll make you feel welcome in her home."

"I just always hate to be a bother."

"You're not bothering anyone, Ma."

"Jessica," I say, but her face crinkles, and I instantly regret calling her by her first name and quickly correct myself. "Ma, Lily's been working on her vision board for her baby's nursery. Maybe you can help her tomorrow to keep your mind occupied."

"A vision board?" Jessica asks, looking confused.

I shrug. "I guess it's the thing to do."

"I'll never understand women today," Thomas says as I move out from under his arm. "Back in my day, we'd just grab a can of paint, splash it on the walls, get a crib, and call it a day."

"You know Lily has to do everything big. She won't be content with some paint," James tells him, and he's speaking the truth.

"Anyway," I say, waving them off. "They have a lovely home on the ocean. If nothing else, you can watch the waves crash on the beach when Lily becomes a little overwhelming."

Jessica smiles genuinely for the first time since we left the compound. "I could get lost in baby land for a little while. It'll help me prepare for my own grandchildren someday."

My stomach drops. She's talking about me birthing those very same grandchildren, and I don't have the heart to tell her it's going to be a while. I'm not ready to have my body double in size, my stomach to be covered in stretch marks, and give up hours upon hours of sleep. On top of that, Mammoth and I need more time together and to get our lives in order before we can bring another life into this world.

"Ma," Mammoth says, warning her, maybe feeling my apprehension. "We still have a few years."

A few years? I was thinking more like a decade, but I'm not sharing that timeline with anyone. I'm pretty sure if Mammoth had his way, I'd already have a tiny human growing inside me.

"Yeah. A few years," I mumble in agreement.

Uncle James laughs, and so does Thomas, getting the evil eye from me.

"We ready?" Uncle Thomas asks after I give them both a heartfelt glare.

Mammoth grabs me by the waist, kissing my forehead. "I'll be right back," he tells me, and I nod as he pulls away. "Come on, Ma. Let's get you settled. It's been a long day." He reaches out to her with his bad arm and instantly winces.

"What's wrong?" she asks immediately.

"Nothing. Just pulled a muscle."

He peers over at me, and my eyes widen. We never called his mom. He wouldn't let us, and she's in the dark that he was shot and is still recovering. I'm not going to be the one to drop the bombshell, but I need to make sure Lily and Jett don't either.

"I'll see you tomorrow, maybe?" Jessica asks me as her son and my uncles walk out of the apartment.

"You will," I tell her, doing whatever it takes to make her feel better about the entire situation.

She smiles before following them out. I don't waste any time taking my phone out of my pocket and dialing Lily.

"Babe."

"Hey," she says, her voice all cheery like always. "What's up? Is Jessica on the way?"

"They just left. They'll be there in under twenty, but I need a huge favor."

"Whatever you want, Tam. You know me."

"You can't tell her about Mammoth being shot."

There's silence instead of a reply.

"Lily, did you hear me?"

"Ohhkay. I'll do my best to not tell her, but you know how I am about secrets."

"Promise me you won't tell her. Promise me you'll do everything in that sweet little heart not to drop that truth nugget on her out of nowhere."

"I promise to do my best."

"Tell your baby daddy too. She can't know. At least not now. She has enough stress on her plate, and I don't want to add to it."

"I'll tell Jett," she says. "We won't tell her. I promise to stay off the subject of last weekend."

"Talk to her about baby shit."

"Baby shit?" Lily asks.

"Yeah. Have her help you with your vision board. She'd like that."

"Are you mocking me?"

"Never," I lie. "I'll come over tomorrow to hang out too. I'll bring lunch or something."

"That would be nice. You can help with the vision board too."

"Fun," I mumble as Gigi peeks her head in the front door, looking around. "I've got to go. Gigi's here."

"Hey, girl!" Lily yells like she's on speakerphone, but she isn't.

"Love you," I tell her.

"You too," she says before I disconnect the call.

"They gone?" Gigi asks, stepping into the small foyer and closing the door behind her.

"Just walked her out. They're in the parking lot, but Mammoth will be back any minute."

I'd already called Gigi and filled her on everything before we left the compound. She told me she'd go to Pike's and stay there for the weekend, but that wasn't really anything new. She was always there, and our place mostly sat empty unless I was home on the weekends.

"Everything go okay?"

I nod. "You know how Uncle James and Thomas are. They handled it all well."

She nods back, smiling. "They've helped us out of more than a few sticky situations."

"When did life get so complicated?" I ask her.

"Cock. It's always a problem."

"No doubt." I laugh.

"Need anything before I head back next door?" She pitches her thumb toward the doorway.

I shake my head. "We're good. I'm exhausted and just want to crawl into bed."

She winks. "I'm sure you do."

I laugh, waving her off. "To sleep. I want to sleep."

She nods. "I'm pretty sure I'll hear all the 'sleeping' going on over here from Pike's bedroom."

"I hear you two too. You're like cats in heat sometimes."

"We're not that loud."

I stare at her and tap my foot, arms crossed, waiting for her to pull that bullshit lie back.

"Whatever. You two aren't quiet either. So…"

"Maybe keep it down a little tonight. I really do plan on sleeping."

She throws up her hands. "Maybe we can borrow your ball gag tonight."

I give her two middle fingers.

She laughs. "I'm out. Bye, babe."

"Bye, girl," I tell her as she opens the door, finding Mammoth on the other side. "Hey, big guy."

"Gigi," he replies, staring down as he towers over her. "You okay?"

"Right as rain," she tells him. "Just heading back to Pike's."

"I don't want to put you out. This is your place."

"Nah. I'm barely ever here. You two have fun tonight," she says, winking at him too. "Don't get too freaky. You still have a bum shoulder. Wouldn't want you to rip out any staples or anything."

Mammoth smirks. "Night, Gigi," he tells her,

ignoring her other comments, which is probably for the best.

"Night, big guy," she says, waving at me before disappearing outside. "Don't do anything I wouldn't do."

"What was that about?" he asks, motioning toward the door when Gigi leaves.

I shrug. "She's just being an idiot and thinks we're going to bump uglies all night."

He scratches his chest, exposing his beautiful stomach and the killer tattoos. "I mean… We can do whatever you want."

"I'm really exhausted," I say, stifling a yawn I've been holding in for the last hour. "Can I get a rain check for the morning?"

"I'm ready for bed too, princess," he tells me as he toes off his boots, placing them next to the door. "This has been the longest day of my life."

I walk up to him, wrapping my arms around his middle, placing my chin on his chest as I gaze up at him. "Are you okay, sparky?"

His hands are on my back, holding my ass. "I am now," he says, bending at the neck and taking my lips along with my exhaustion.

TAMARA'S STANDING OVER ME, holding my phone way too close to my face. "What's the number you keep ignoring?"

I blink a few times, trying to focus on the screen. "Nothing important."

She raises an eyebrow, placing one hand on her hip. "Then, can I answer it?"

"No."

She raises her hand, ready to press the button even though I told her not to.

"It's the physical therapy place," I finally tell her because the woman can't mind her own business to save her life.

"Why aren't you answering? You need to make an appointment."

"I don't need an appointment. I don't need

therapy. My shoulder is already healing and feels better every day." I lift my shoulder, moving it around, and avoid wincing even though there's an awkward and searing pain shooting down my arm. "See."

She places the phone on the table and crawls into my lap, straddling my legs. "Why are men so hardheaded?"

"I'm not being difficult. I know my body, princess. It's nothing a little hard work and use won't fix. I don't need to go to a doctor's office and do stretching exercises while paying them hundreds of dollars for shit I can fix on my own."

Tamara scoots closer, smashing her tits against my chest. "You've been good at hiding it from your mother, I'll give you that. But I see you wince and pull back from the pain."

"There's no reason to make her worry about something that's in the past. I'm on the road to recovery, and she has enough on her plate right now. I don't need to add to it."

She nods, dipping her face closer. "I won't tell her. I also won't force you to go to therapy, but if you don't get better and get more use from your shoulder, promise me you'll go to one appointment and get it checked out," she begs.

"I promise if it doesn't heal in the next few weeks, I'll call them and go in. I have to go to the surgeon next week to have them take the staples out."

Tamara grimaces. "Sounds like a great time."

"It'll feel better to get them out. They're constantly tugging and itching, baby. They bother me more than the wound itself."

My phone rings again, and Tamara turns her head to the side, looking at the screen. "It's Thomas."

"Answer it," I tell her, keeping my hands on her back, resting just above her ass.

Tamara taps the screen and says, "Hey, Uncle."

"Tam, is Mammoth there?"

"You're on speaker, and we're both here," she tells him, staring at me. "Everything okay?"

"I made some calls this morning," he sighs. "It hasn't been easy."

"Fuck," I mutter, closing my eyes.

"Don't worry. We found enough skeletons in his closet that it won't matter what people think of him. Give us the rest of the day, and everything should be cleared tomorrow. James and I are coming up with the best plan and taking the steps to carry it out as quickly as possible. Just sit tight and let us do what we do best."

Tamara smiles, wrapping her arms around my neck, resting her hands on the chair back behind me. "I can keep you busy," she mouths, smirking.

"Thanks, Thomas. I appreciate everything you two are doing to help my mom. I know you didn't—"

"Don't say it. We've told you this before. Told Pike

the same thing. You may not have been born into this family, but you're still part of it. You're one of us. I know if I needed you, you'd have my back in a heartbeat."

"Hell yeah, I would," I tell him without hesitation or doubt. "Whatever you need, I'm there. Is there anything I can do to help right now? Anything at all?"

"Nothing. We got this. Just make sure your mom stays low. Lily said she'd keep her busy and not let her out of the house, but you know how forceful Lily is when faced with confrontation."

"We'll head over there in a bit," Tamara tells him, "and make sure she stays out of sight, Uncle."

"Thanks, doll. I'll call soon with an update," he says. "Talk later."

"Bye."

"Thanks," I say before he has a chance to end the call, but there's no reply before my screen goes blank.

"You wanna go now?" Tamara asks me, fingers dug into my hair, toying with the sensitive skin on the back of my neck.

I curl my fingers, gripping her ass rougher. "Princess, there's only one thing I want right now, and it's sitting right in my lap." I lean forward, pressing my lips against her neck.

Tamara tips her head back, exposing her neck as she grinds against my cock. "Everything else can wait," she whispers, yanking my hair forward and holding my lips against her skin.

I lick the flesh near her ear, peppering her neck with kisses and making a trail to her cleavage. "I always miss your body when we're apart," I murmur.

"Just my body?"

"Not just your body. Everything about you. Your attitude. Your fierceness. Your warmth. Your love."

"That was sweet, sparky," she says, inching her body even closer until there's no space left between us. "But how about less talking and more licking?"

I growl, sinking my teeth into her soft skin, causing her to squeak. "You want it rough, princess, or you want me to love you softly?"

She tips her head forward, bringing her lips near mine. "Hard. I want it hard," she says, sliding her hand between her legs and groping my cock. "Really hard."

"Hard," I repeat, my voice almost cracking because she already has my cock straining for relief.

Tamara's fingers work the button and zipper of my jeans, showing me just how hungry she is. I stand, hands under her ass, carrying her out of the small kitchen to the couch. I set her down and straighten, pulling my T-shirt over my head and tossing it to the floor.

She watches, eyes blazing with fire, licking her lips.

"The pants too," she whispers, gaze dipping toward my undone jeans.

As I push my jeans down, Tamara lifts her ass, slipping out of her tiny shorts before lifting her tank top over her head and tossing her clothes to the floor next to mine.

I stand there naked, cock at full attention, soaking her in as she lies back on the couch, legs spread, looking like a sex goddess. "Put your mouth on me again," she says, sliding her hand between her legs, teasing me. "I want to taste myself on your lips when you kiss me."

Fuck. She's absolutely perfect. I drop to my knees, lifting her leg and placing it over my good shoulder before bringing my mouth to her pussy and feasting like a starving man. My lips are covering her, face buried, when the front door opens and there's a familiar shriek.

Tamara's eyes widen and her body stiffens, but I keep my face where it is, figuring I'm at least covering her body with my mouth, which is better than nothing.

"Fuck!" Gigi screams before slamming the door, going back outside.

"Jesus," Tamara mutters, lifting up on her elbows, tits glistening in the morning sun, and laughing softly. "She's a buzzkill sometimes."

I pull away, licking her wetness from my lips but

staying on the floor, hiding my dick in case Gigi decides to make an appearance again.

"Do that shit in your bedroom. Not in the living room! I eat dinner on that couch!" Gigi's still yelling outside, and Tamara's rolling her eyes.

"Go back to Pike's!" Tamara yells back, not moving from the couch. "We're not done yet."

"I don't have time to wait while you two bang for hours. I need some things in my room. You have thirty seconds to get yourself out of the living room before I walk in there and see you both fully naked."

"She's already seen me naked," Tamara tells me, still not fucking moving.

"She hasn't seen me," I reply.

"She might like what she sees and finally realize what a real man looks like." She waggles her eyebrows. "She'd probably have a heart attack and die if she saw the size of your cock."

"Fifteen seconds!" Gigi screams.

I leave our clothes and grab Tamara off the couch with one arm, tossing her over my shoulder. "She ain't seeing my dick, princess."

Tamara's thin fingers find my ass, pinching my cheeks. "I'd have that thing as my screen saver if I could."

I grunt, swatting at her pretty little ass. "No pictures either," I tell her as I stalk down the hallway, carrying her into her bedroom.

"Too late," she says, laughing as I kick the door closed, giving us privacy. "I have more pictures of your dick than your face."

"How?" I ask, tossing her onto the bed.

She squeals, grabbing on to the comforter as she bounces. "You sleep naked, Saint. You sleep hard, and I take advantage of that time to take some photos for my spank bank when I'm away at school."

I stand at the end of the bed, looming over her, my cock still hard as fuck even if Gigi walked in and saw more than I ever wanted her to. "You love my cock that much?"

"It's your best feature."

I slide between her open legs and hover above her, staring down at her beautiful face. "I should be offended by that statement, but I'm not."

She reaches down, grabbing my cock, pumping the length in her fist. "It's not why I love you, but it's just so damn pretty."

"My manhood should never be called pretty."

Tamara chuckles, still stroking my dick. "It's a work of art. I'd frame it if I could."

"Baby, stop talking," I grit out. "Put my cock in you."

She smiles, gripping tighter as I move closer, lining up our bodies. When she guides my cock to her pussy, her hand falls away and I push inside, feeling at home again as the pleasure of her body wrapped around me settles in deep.

I take her lips, soaking in her moans as I slide my length in and out of her over and over again. She locks her ankles around my ass, holding me to her and meeting my thrusts. She moves her hands to my lower back, digging her nails into my skin and sending shock waves of pleasure and pain throughout my body.

I kiss her rougher, pump harder, stroke her deeper until my one good arm is shaking and our bodies are covered in sweat.

She breaks our kiss, staring up at me with her nails still in my skin but her ankles falling away from my body. "Roll over," she says, being bossy and taking control, which at times, I more than fucking love.

I roll to my back, taking Tamara with me, my cock still buried deep inside her. She straddles me, back straight, tits pushed out and on full display. She's absolutely beautiful. Every inch of her light-brown skin shimmers in the sunlight streaming through the bedroom windows. Her hazel eyes shine with so much fire and hunger, I'm more than happy to sit back and enjoy the ride.

She rests her hands on my chest, gripping my biceps as leverage as she starts to grind on me, pressing her pretty pussy against me. "So fuckin' deep," she moans. "So fuckin' good."

"Ride me, princess." I grab her hip with one

hand, using my other to toy with her nipples. "Show me how you like it."

She plants her feet on either side of my hips, lifting her middle from my body, careful to keep just the tip of me inside. With all her might, she slams down on me, gasping when I fill every inch of her until there's nowhere left to go.

I force myself to keep my eyes open, watching her pleasure herself, using me the way she wants for her own satisfaction.

I could do this for a lifetime and never get sick of her. I could do this forever and still want more. I could do this for an eternity and feel like, somehow, it wasn't long enough.

She curls her fingers into my chest, nails biting into my skin as she rides my cock so roughly her breasts bounce, but I don't move, letting her suck every ounce of pleasure out of me.

"Oh God, yes," she moans, rocking against me harder than before, squeezing her hazel eyes shut as she falls over the cliff, chasing her orgasm.

When she collapses forward, I roll us over until she's on her back and I'm on top of her again. I lift her leg, pounding into her, finding the rhythm I need to achieve the same release.

I collapse onto my side, rolling onto my back again, Tamara next to me. The only sounds in the apartment are our gasps for air, as we try to steady our breathing and fail.

"This is the best way to start a day," she says, still breathing heavy. "May can't come soon enough."

No truer words have ever been spoken. I am ready to start our life together. I've finally gained as much freedom as I can from the club, but now it is a matter of waiting for her to graduate until we can have this every morning and be there for each other every day.

"I know, princess," I whisper into her hair as she curls in next to my side. "It'll be here before you know it."

"I was thinking about what you asked earlier." She peers up at me, hand on my chest, hair flowing over my arm. "I think we should try it."

"Yeah?" I ask, wondering which thing I asked her about earlier that she is finally agreeing to.

"I want to work with you. I want to build something together."

My smile is immediate and unstoppable. "Just when I think life can't get any better, you find a way to make me even happier."

"I'm still not living above the garage, though," she replies without so much as a smirk.

"No garage for you. You deserve the best."

She closes her eyes, humming her approval, and moments later, we both drift off to sleep.

CHAPTER
SIXTEEN
TAMARA

LILY YELLS for us to come in, but as soon as I walk into the living room, I freeze, and Mammoth bumps into my back.

"What are you doing?" I ask, staring at Jessica and Lily as they sit near the coffee table. They're surrounded by hundreds of little pieces of paper cut out of dozens of magazines that are scattered around the floor, glue sticks everywhere, and a few pairs of scissors.

"We're working on our vision boards," Lily says, not even looking up from her work.

"Our?" I ask as Mammoth steps around me to get a better look at their new art project.

"Yeah." Lily looks up and smiles, holding a glue stick. "Jessica wanted to make one too. So, *we* have been working on *ours* all afternoon."

"Ma, what the hell is this?" Mammoth asks as he stands over them, staring down at the big white boards on the floor.

Jessica peers up, tucking her legs farther underneath herself, with a cut-out picture of something in her hand. "My dreams for the future, honey."

Mammoth's eyes scan the poster board, and I creep closer out of sheer curiosity. "It's filled with babies," he says, and my eyes widen.

"Are you going to have another baby?" I whisper to Jessica, shocked by the dozens of little babies and all the baby things glued down around them.

"No, sweetie. You are," she replies, and my belly flips at the ease with which she says those words.

"I...I..." I stammer, feeling winded and unable to think, let alone form a complete sentence.

She's wishing into life grandbabies—and lots of them. Not just a few, but she literally has dozens of them in all different skin shades, looking all cute and happy.

"Aren't they beautiful?" she asks us, looking from me to Mammoth when I don't reply because my mouth is gaping open and no words are coming out.

"I think you have about twenty too many, Ma."

Jessica laughs and presses another baby to her board, smiling the entire time. "One can never have too many babies. My biggest regret in life is only having one child. I wish you had at least one brother or sister. Someone besides me to lean on. If I could get a do-over, that would be the one thing I'd change."

Mammoth runs his fingers through his hair, exasperated. "I'm fine, and I'm not alone anymore. I have Tamara, Lily, and all the Gallos."

"That makes me so happy," she tells him as she shifts the paper around on the floor, searching for something. "I'm so glad you found such a wonderful family filled with so much love and so many people."

"She's putting another baby on the board," I whisper to Mammoth, transfixed by what she's doing and unable to look away.

Mammoth reaches behind his back, finding my hand and giving it a light squeeze. "Tamara and I will start a family someday, but first, we have a business to start."

"Life is about more than money," Jessica says, peering up from the board again. "Don't wait too long. You're not getting any younger."

Jett walks into the room from the back of the house, ignoring the fact that Lily and Jessica have made a complete mess of the living room. "Hey, guys," he greets us. "The ladies have been busy."

"See that," Mammoth deadpans.

"Can I talk to you for a minute?" he asks Mammoth, ticking his chin upward. "Outside."

"Go," I tell Mammoth. "I got this."

"You sure?" he asks over his shoulder before turning to face me.

I nod. "I've had a lifetime of Lily. I can easily handle Jessica too."

Mammoth gives me a smile. "I have no doubt you can handle anything thrown your way, princess."

I smile back, popping up on my tiptoes to give him a kiss. "Go," I say softly. "I'll be fine."

He gives my hand another light squeeze as he returns my kiss. "I'll only be a minute," he says and then follows Jett out the sliding doors lining the back of the house.

"Come sit," Lily says, pointing to the one free spot near them that isn't covered by paper. "I can get you a board too."

"I'm good," I reply as I plop down on the floor, watching them like they're one peanut short of a Snickers bar. "I keep all the inspiration I need up here." I tap my temple.

Lily laughs, shaking her head at me. "You're crazy."

"Yeah," I mutter, rolling my eyes. "I'm the crazy one in this trio." I scan Jessica's board again, finally seeing other things besides all the little cherubic, happy babies scattered everywhere. "Are you going to go back north?"

Jessica sets down her glue stick and leans back against the front of the couch. "I don't think I want to go back. Too many bad memories and I don't have a house to go back to now that I sold the one I loved."

"That has to be hard."

"It is, but maybe it's for the better. I think it's time for me to live closer to my son again. And now, he has you, and someday, you two will get married and give me grandbabies."

"Not dozens, though," I correct her, and she smiles.

"Even if it's one grandbaby, I don't want to miss a moment of their life."

"We'll have more than one."

Her smile widens. "You've made this old lady's day."

"You're hardly old."

"I had Josiah when I was young. We weren't even twenty when we got pregnant. We were married and living in base housing, trying to fit six months' worth of sex into a short time period because he was about to be deployed."

"Well, you two had to be busy, then." I cover my mouth, laughing.

"They were some great times." Jessica winks at

me. "But we were probably too young to have a baby. I did the best I could."

My heart aches for her. It's been decades since she lost her husband, and the pain is still etched all over her face when she speaks about him.

"I'm sorry," I whisper.

"I didn't think I'd be in my early twenties and be a widow." She brushes her brown hair back and away from her shoulders as her face grows more serious. "He gave me one beautiful, strong son. I don't regret my life or my choices. I'm glad we had Josiah when we did, or else I would've been alone. The only way I made it through those dark days was with the happy, smiling face of my baby boy."

I gaze down at the papers, moving them aside with the backs of my fingers. I can't look at her. She says she's fine, but the pain I can easily see is too much for me in that moment after what just happened to Mammoth. "I can only imagine."

"I think, if it's okay with you, I should find a place to live nearby, so I can be there for Josiah, you, and someday, my grandbabies."

"It's totally fine with me." I smile, finding a photo of the beautiful Florida sunset across the Gulf and handing it to her. "I think you'll like it here."

She takes the paper, staring at the colors. "I've never lived by the ocean."

"There's nothing more beautiful," Lily tells her, leaning over to get a better look at the photo in Jessica's hand. "We take it for granted because we grew up with it nearby, but the sound of the waves and the technicolor sunsets over the Gulf are the most spectacular sight in the world."

"Are there any condos on the water around here? I don't want to deal with a yard, and I could use some easiness in my life right now."

"There're tons of condos, and a few are on the water. I have a friend who's a real estate agent. I'll give you her number, and she'll find you whatever you want."

The barely visible lines near Jessica's eyes become more distinct as she smiles. "I'd love that, Lily. You're truly one of the sweetest human beings I've ever met."

"I wish I were going to be around to house hunt with you," I tell her, hating that I have to go back to college.

"Honey—" Jessica reaches across the paper and grabs my hand "—college is important. I've bought and sold more houses in my life than you've bought cars. I'll be just fine doing it on my own."

"Josiah will help," Lily says, snickering. "I'm sure Josiah won't let you do it alone." I can tell she loves saying his name because ever since she found out his real name, she can't stop using it.

When I called Lily earlier, she said Josiah no less than twenty times. It was only obvious because she overused it and kept doing so until I hung up, finally over her giggle fits every time. The conversation took twice as long because she was practically hysterical.

"I prefer to house hunt alone. I don't need the input of a man, especially not my son. I want what I want and won't allow anyone to talk me out of my dreams anymore."

I exhale, slowly blinking as a smile spreads across my face. "I like how you think," I say to her, getting a small smile in return.

"The older you get, the less you care about other people's opinions, honey. You'll see."

"Tamara has never cared what others think about her or what she does. She's the rebel in the family."

"Ah," Jessica whispers, "just like my son. He always had to do things his way or not at all."

"That ain't no shit," I mumble.

"How's his shoulder?" Lily asks, placing a photo of a crib on her board, not even looking at me as my eyes almost bug out of my head. "Is it almost healed?"

"What's wrong with his shoulder?" Jessica asks immediately, placing the paper and scissors she'd just picked up back down on the floor.

"Nothing," I shoot back just as fast as she asked.

"What aren't you telling me?" She narrows her eyes, studying my face, trying to read my expression.

"He's fine. He just tweaked it doing some work," I lie, thinking I covered pretty well.

But Jessica's eyes sweep across my face as her lips twist. "You're a shit liar, honey. I won't hold that against you, but someone better tell me the truth about my son and do it quick."

"He was shot last weekend," I blurt out, feeling the weight of her stare and hating the idea of lying to such a sweet person. "But he's okay and almost healed."

"Shit. I forgot," Lily whispers, shaking her head. "Sorry." She gives me a sorrowful smile, getting a curled lip in response.

"He what?" Jessica pales, covering her mouth with her hand. "He was shot? You just said he was shot, yeah? I'm not hearing things, am I? My mind didn't switch words? He was shot, and no one bothered to call me and tell me about it?"

"He didn't want you to worry. He forbade me from calling you. I'm sorry. I'm so, so, so, so sorry, Jessica."

"Ma," she corrects me.

Damn it. Calling her Ma is still so foreign, and I know it's probably going to take me years to get used to calling her Ma instead of Jessica, no matter how hard I try.

"You know how your son is. He's always so private."

"Was it an accident?" she asks me on the spot.

"Kind of."

"If you call getting shot by another motorcycle club accidental, then yes," Lily says casually as she cuts out something from her *Mommy and Me* magazine. "I'm sure they didn't mean to put a slug in his shoulder as he sat outside the strip club."

I glare at Lily, ready to crawl across the floor and jam some of the scraps into her mouth just to shut her up.

"What?" Jessica screeches as her body goes rigid.

"He's out of the club," I assure Jessica. "When you showed up at the compound, it was his last night there. He left because of me and is setting up his own business over here. We're going to start a new life away from the danger and bullshit that comes from being in an MC like the Disciples. Don't worry about him anymore. They're not an issue."

The guys walk back into the house at that very moment, Mammoth scratching his stomach and Jett checking his phone.

Mammoth's gaze swings from me to his mother, noticing the freaking crazy-high amount of tension in the room. "What happened?"

Jessica crosses her arms, dropping a shoulder, throwing tons of attitude before she even opens her mouth. "You have something to tell me?"

His eyes come to me, and I cringe, tipping my head toward Lily because we all know she can't keep a secret worth shit. "Um," Mammoth mutters. "No."

"Nothing at all?" Jessica asks again, lips twisted so tightly her entire face is distorted.

He shrugs. "I mean, we were just talking to James, and things are almost done."

Jessica climbs to her feet and stalks toward her son. She lifts her hand like she's about to punch him square in the shoulder, but he moves to the side.

"What the hell, Ma?" he asks her, eyebrows furrowed.

"Me, what the hell?" she repeats, hand still in the air, head tipped back, glaring up at her son. "How about someone has a hole in his body, but no one bothered to tell me about the fact that my son was lying in a hospital bed somewhere, fighting for his life."

"Oh fuck," Jett whispers, eyes moving from his phone to Lily. "What did you do?" he mouths.

She covers her face, shaking her head, hiding out because she knows she fucked up. "Pregnancy brain," she whispers, using it as a great excuse because who can be mad at the pregnant lady?

Mammoth reaches out and grabs Jessica's hand that she still looks like she's about to strike him with. "It wasn't that bad, Ma. My shoulder is almost healed and like its old shit self. Wasn't the first time I've been shot, but hopefully it'll be the last."

I slap myself on the forehead. A man's ability to explain shit never seems to make a woman feel any better about the situation. Reminding his mother that he's been shot before probably wasn't the best course of action, but he said it anyway.

"Hopefully?" Her voice is high-pitched and squeaky. "I've never been shot. People don't usually get shot. It's not a thing most people do or get, Josiah. Lily—" Jessica turns toward my cousin "—have you been shot?"

I close my eyes, muttering a few curse words as Lily says, "No."

"Jett?" Jessica asks, moving her eyes to him.

"A few times," he says, like it's not a big deal because he's a man filled with testosterone and lunacy. "Military, ma'am."

"And outside the military?" she asks a second later, tapping her foot.

"No, and I'm hoping to keep it that way, but in my line of work, anything's possible."

"You need a new job," Lily says quietly at my side.

"Tamara, have you been shot?" she asks me next, and I can't lie.

"No, Ma. I've never been shot."

"Most people have never been shot or shot at, Josiah. And when they do get a bullet in their body, they usually call their mother because it's the right thing to do. I would've come down here sooner. I would've been at your side, making sure you were healing right. It's my job as your mother to make sure my baby is taken care of."

Mammoth lifts both arms, placing his big hands on her shoulders, and doesn't grimace with the motion. "Tamara nursed me back to health. She took good care of me, Ma, and I didn't want you to worry. I know how you get."

He pauses for a second and I think he's almost done, but then he keeps rolling just as his mom was about to open her mouth.

"You didn't tell me about Boyd hitting you. It's just as bad, if not worse. Looks like we've both been keeping secrets, but it stops today. Total transparency from now on. Understand?"

"A fresh start," she whispers, gazing up at her son, who's no longer a little boy, but a grown man. "No more secrets. No more lies."

"No more, Ma, but this has to be a two-way street. Okay?"

She nods. "Total transparency. No bullshit."

"No bullshit," he repeats. "From here on out, we're nothing but honest."

"Good." She smiles and lifts her hand to his face, cradling his cheek. "I hate the beard."

"What?" he asks.

"While we're being honest, I'm telling you, I hate the beard."

I gasp. "Oh my God," I whisper. "Do not shave it off. Please. Please. Please do not shave it off."

"Beard's staying, Ma. My woman loves it."

Jessica shrugs and laughs softly. "I was just starting the total honesty thing with something simple."

I exhale, feeling relieved. "Thank God," I mutter under my breath, clutching my chest.

"Maybe we don't have to be honest and transparent about *everything*."

She laughs louder. "No. I suppose we don't, but the important things, the life-and-death things, can't be hidden any longer."

He nods, wrapping his arms around her as she moves in to embrace him. "I love you, Josiah."

"Love you too, Ma," he whispers in her hair like he does to me.

I smile, staring at the two of them like a lovestruck idiot. I love this rough and tough man, and I love the way he loves his mother.

You can tell a lot about a man by how he treats and respects the woman who gave him life. I'm not saying every mother is worthy of love and kindness, because I know there're a lot of shit parents out there. But Jessica is good people, and Mammoth loves her, respects her, and would do anything to protect her.

That's all I need to know about him to understand he will do the same for me and our someday babies.

My belly flips at the thought.

Damn.

I don't know if I'll ever be ready to be a mom, but I have a feeling it is going to happen sooner rather than later if Jessica has her way.

JETT HANDS me a beer and sits down at the table across from me. "James and Thomas are on their way here."

I stare out across the Gulf of Mexico, watching the waves rise and fall, lapping at the shore. "Good. I hope the shit's settled."

"They didn't sound like anything went wrong, but you know they like to deliver family news in person and not over the phone." Jett takes a sip of his beer, relaxing back into his chair. "We're damn lucky to have them in our lives. Hell, to have the entire family."

"That's no lie," I tell him, tipping my beer in his direction and looking his way. "I can't thank you enough for taking my mother in last night."

"Are you kidding me? She's kept Lily busy. I

should be the one thanking you for giving me a mental baby break."

"You doin' okay?" I ask, genuinely curious because he's said very little about their pregnancy.

I don't think the reality has really sunk in yet. He found out, spilled the news to her parents, and then came to my rescue, watching me get shot. Who could process all that in such a short amount of time? I know I couldn't.

"I think I am. I mean—" he rubs the back of his neck "—it's not like I have a choice, but I know I'm happy. I'm excited, actually, but I know it's not going to be as fun as my imagination is allowing me to believe."

I laugh. "At least you'll have a lot of babysitters. There will be no shortage of people who will be more than willing to take the baby off your hands for several hours."

"I figure they'll fight over the baby. It'll be a win-win for everybody. We'll get some alone time and maybe a few nights' sleep here and there, and they'll get baby time."

"First grandchild. Never thought Lily would be the one to do it. Figured Gigi would get knocked up before anybody else."

"I don't think Gigi's ready to be a mother."

"I know Tamara isn't either."

"Lily will make a great mom," he says, staring off into the distance like I had been.

"She will be the best mom," I tell him.

Tamara pops her head out of the sliding glass door. "The guys are here."

Jett stands and I follow, moving into the house to hear whatever they have to say about the Boyd situation. Hopefully, they've found a way to clear my mother so she can get back to living instead of being under the thumb of an abusive asshole for defending herself.

Thomas is standing in the living room, holding my mother's hands, greeting her. James is behind him, hugging Lily.

"Hey," Thomas says, tipping his chin my way when he finally moves his gaze away from my mother.

"Hey," I reply.

"Why don't we sit?" James says, letting go of Lily and motioning toward the sitting area. "We have a lot to talk about."

I sit down next to my mother, and Tamara sits on the other side of me. Jett moves into the recliner, pulling Lily into his lap and wrapping his arms around her middle. James and Thomas stay standing, never willing to relax even for a minute. It's like they're ready to run out the door or expect bad shit to happen every second of every day.

"We dug up everything we could about Boyd

Weaver, and let me tell you, there was a lot," Thomas says, speaking first. "Decades' worth of information, and barely any of it was him doing good."

I curl my hand into a fist, and my mother places her palm over my fingers, always watchful of every movement I make, even when it has to do with her life.

James rubs his hands together as he spread his legs, standing with his feet shoulder-width apart. "He had connections, but we were finally able to get around all the bullshit. We spoke to the sheriff in the town where there was a warrant out for you."

James said "was," and with those words, I exhale, knowing everything is settled.

"You aren't the first woman Boyd has laid hands on, Jessica. He's done it before, but you were the first one who fought back," James tells my mom, staring down at her with nothing but kindness in his green eyes.

"Anyway," Thomas says, interrupting James. "Long story short, the charges have been completely dropped, and you'll never have to worry about Boyd again."

"What do you mean, I don't have to worry about him again?" Ma whispers, squeezing my hand. "Is he dead?"

I almost laugh because she's probably thinking we killed him at the compound, but we didn't. He walked away with his other arm broken, but he was breathing.

"There was an old Florida warrant out for him from the eighties. By him coming here and going to the authorities about what transpired at the Disciples' compound, he left himself open for arrest. He's currently in lockup with no bail. Based on his crimes and his running forty years ago, I'm thinking he's going away for a very long time."

"Oh, dear God," Ma whispers again. "What did he do?"

"Assault and battery, trespassing, property damage, and attempted murder."

Ma squeezes my hand harder. "Jesus. I never would've thought he was a bad guy."

"Until he hit you the first time," I mutter, earning me a stern look telling me to zip my lips.

"He really was sweet to me," she explains. "Nothing but a true gentleman…until he wasn't, and by then, it was too late."

"He was nothing but a liar," I reply. "The people who seem the sweetest are sometimes the most evil, Ma. No one is who they appear to be, but only who they allow you to see."

James shifts and digs a tiny slip of paper out of his pocket, handing it to my mother. "Here's the sheriff's name and number. If you have any issues, you call me or Thomas, and if we're busy, call him immediately."

"Thank you," Ma says with relief in her voice. "I owe you so much."

Thomas shakes his head. "You're Mammoth's mom, and since he's now family, so are you. We take care of our family. We protect our family. And we'd do anything for one another. There's no thanks necessary, and you don't owe us a thing, ma'am."

Ma stands, releasing my hand, and walks toward Thomas and James. "May I?" she asks, opening her arms. "I know you don't want a payment, but I'd love a hug."

"I'm sure she does," Tamara whispers, elbowing me in the ribs.

"Stop," I grumble, watching as my mother hugs Thomas, taking her sweet-ass time doing it too. "She's my mother."

"She's hot, though," Tamara continues to tell me. "Some man is going to snap her up and make her his."

I turn, staring at my girl, who's grinning like a crazy person as she watches my mother move on to James. "You're talking about my mom, princess."

Tamara nods. "I know, but you're going to have to get over that fact. She's still young and a looker. Men are going to be tripping over their tongues to get a piece of her."

I close my eyes, controlling my breathing. "Are you trying to kill me?"

Tamara laughs, slapping my leg. "I'm sure she dated when you were a kid."

"Nope," I clip, opening my eyes again to look at Tamara. "She never dated, at least not that I knew, until I moved out and joined the military."

"All those years wasted," Tamara whispers and sits up a little straighter as my ma walks back toward us. "She has lost time to make up for. So, buckle up, sparky. It's going to be a wild ride."

I lift my gaze upward toward the ceiling and groan. "What a fucking nightmare."

"What's wrong, honey?" Ma asks, touching my shoulder as she sits back down next to me. "You don't look happy."

"Nothing," I snap.

"He gets cranky sometimes," Tamara tells her, patting my leg. "I'm sure you know how he is."

"I could tell you some stories that would make your head spin." Ma smiles.

"Later, I'll open a bottle of wine, and maybe you can share some of them with me," Tamara says, leaning her head on my shoulder, laughing quietly. "I've only known him as this grumpy guy, and I want to know more about the little, cranky boy."

"We're going to take off," James says, pitching his thumb toward the door. "If you don't need anything else."

"We're good," I say, standing up, needing a

minute away from Tamara and my ma. "I'll walk you two out."

Thomas nods and hugs Lily before moving toward the door with James and me behind him.

"I can't thank you two enough. Really, whatever you need, I'm there," I tell them, offering my hand to Thomas when he stops near his car.

He shakes with one hand and grabs my good shoulder with his other. "We meant what we said in there. We're family. This is what we do. For good or bad, you're one of us now."

"There's only good," I reply as he releases my hand.

James lifts his hand, slapping me on the back, not giving a single fuck how much pain it causes me. "Take care of our niece and treat her well. That's payment enough."

"I'll do that," I grit out as the pain from my shoulder starts to wane quicker than it has in days.

James lifts his hand from my shoulder and backs up, moving toward the car. "See you tomorrow," he says, smiling. "Bring your mom. I know the family would love to meet her."

"I will," I tell him, giving him a chin lift as they open the car doors, ready to climb inside.

"Everything okay, honey?" Ma asks, sneaking up on me.

"Everything is fine, Ma." I glance down at her in

her sundress as she covers her eyes, shading them from the sun. "Is the entire family this good-looking?"

I laugh and nod. "Pretty much."

"Are they all that kind?"

"Completely."

She wraps an arm around my center, placing her hand on my waist and resting her head against my bicep. "You did well, baby. Real well."

"I don't know if I deserve her or this entire family."

Ma places her other hand on my chest, over my heart. "You deserve every bit of this," she tells me, sounding sweet and sure. "I always wanted a big family for you. One that cared about you as much as I do, and I think you found it."

"Just dumb fucking luck."

She pulls her head away, peering up at me. "Doesn't matter how they came into your life. All that matters is that you hold on tight and never let go."

"Wise words, Ma."

She gives me a pat. "Just reality, honey. Now, let's go back in there. I have my vision board to finish while I figure out where to go next and what to do with my newfound freedom."

"You can stay with me," I offer.

"With those men and all the scantily clad women?"

I laugh, throwing my arm around my mom's

shoulder and guiding her back to Lily and Jett's house. "No. I left the club. Today's my first official day of freedom too."

She stops walking, giving me her eyes again. "You really left the club for good?"

"Yeah."

"Like forever forever?" she asks in disbelief.

"Yeah."

"You sure it's gonna stick?"

"Yeah, Ma. This time was the right time. I met the woman of my dreams, Ma, and she isn't about that life. I've been planning my exit since the day Tamara walked into my life, and that day finally arrived."

She curls into me, squeezing my waist tightly. "You've made me so happy. Some nights I couldn't sleep when I thought about you doing…"

"They're not all bad people," I correct her. I'm not going to win the argument. She's seen one too many television shows about motorcycle clubs, and no matter what I say, she isn't going to change her mind. "It's in the past now."

She smiles as she gazes up at me. "You've made me happier today than you have in a long time."

"I always want to make you proud and make sure you're happy."

"You know what'll make me happy, honey?" she asks, smiling all sweet and innocent.

I know what's going to come out of her mouth

before she says the words. Based on her vision board, the only thing that'll make her happy is grandbabies and lots of them. "What'll make you happy, Ma?"

"Whatever makes you happy," she replies, shocking me.

"Not grandbabies?"

Her smile widens. "Those too, but in due time. You're young and have plenty of time to give me lots of grandkids. For now, I want you to enjoy life, enjoy your girlfriend, and enjoy being young. Life flies by in the blink of an eye and should be savored as much as possible. Live life on your own timeline. Not on mine."

I pull her against my chest, hugging her, and kissing her forehead. "Thanks, Ma. I want you to find your happy also. You're still young too."

She laughs. "You're precious."

"Just don't find that happiness with someone I know, please. I'm not sure I can handle that."

She nods. "Got it. So, any complete stranger will do. Duly noted."

Shit.

I didn't think that through.

Clearly, her ability to pick the right man is off after her time with Boyd, but I also know I don't want her with someone I am close to like Morris. He is too young for her, and the cougar jokes would get real old pretty fucking quick. One of us wouldn't come out the other end alive.

"Maybe you should just keep things casual for a while, no matter who you date."

"I like casual," she tells me, and my stomach twists because she's my mom and we're talking about dating, therefore, sex.

"Just nothing serious. Don't run off and move in with the first guy who looks like a good thing."

This time, she guides me toward the house. "Honey," she says, and I've always loved how sweet that word sounded coming from her lips, "I'm not looking to jump back into something so serious. Maybe if we would've casually dated for a while, I would've seen the other side of him. I do know, the next time I'm really interested in someone, I'll probably call Tamara's uncles and have them run a background check on him."

"That's not a bad idea," I tell her because it's not. Some simple checking on Boyd and a million little red flags would've been waving in her face, sending her in the opposite direction.

"And I'll have you around too. You have a pretty good sense about people, especially men."

"So, you're sticking around for more than a little while?"

She nods as we stand in the doorway. "I have nowhere to go back to, and it's about time I stick close to my son and his girl, waiting on those grandbabies who will eventually come."

"But not too soon," I remind her.

"Not too soon." She smiles back. "Now, let's celebrate. I'm no longer a wanted criminal. That calls for a drink."

I laugh and shake my head, never thinking I'd hear those words coming out of my mother's mouth and hoping I never do again.

EIGHT MONTHS *later*

I stare at myself in the full-length mirror, smiling like an idiot. I never thought this day would come. It always felt so far away and elusive, but somehow, I survived the last four years to make it to college graduation day. The cap and gown are hideous, but they're part of the rite of passage. At least it's not the same awful color that I had to wear during my high school ceremony, but it is still no more flattering.

"Let me see my baby," my mom says, walking into my apartment on campus without even knocking.

"Oh my God!" I scream, clutching my chest as my heart hammers so fast you'd think I'd just walked out of a haunted house. "You scared the shit out of me."

"You knew we'd be here. You're such a drama queen." My mother waves me off before she grabs my shoulders, gawking at me in my cap and gown. "I never thought this day would come. I'm so stinking proud. Let me see you."

"You look all grown up," Dad says, walking in a few seconds after her with my brother Asher next to him.

"Yo," my little brother says, looking not so small anymore. He's as tall as my father, but bulkier, like a football player and not a musician.

Sadly for my father, my brother doesn't have a musical bone in his body. He sings every song off-key and can't follow a beat to save his life. So, instead of molding him into becoming the next big rock star, Dad pushed him into athletics, and my brother excels at using his muscles and not so much of his creative brain. He is still in high school, but he's a rising star on the basketball and football teams.

My parents spend their weeknights at games, cheering on their son, which is fine by me because if they have their eyes on him, they aren't watching me so closely.

Not that I am ever doing anything wrong. I just don't need them all up in my business every second of every day. They've given me room to breathe over the years, but without Asher, I'm pretty sure I wouldn't have had as much freedom or anonymity.

"Hey," I tell him, giving him the same chin lift he gave me when he walked in.

"I need to get photos," Ma says, ignoring my short and stunted conversation with my brother. "This is a big day."

I pull on the sides of my gown, showing my mother just how stupidly large the thing is. "I look like you could put a string on me and fly me in the air like a kite."

Asher laughs as he pulls out his phone, staring down at his screen, already bored with the entire day.

Dad elbows him and gives him a stern and somehow laughable glare. Dad likes to play a good game, acting like he is somehow tough as a parent, but he isn't. Mom is the one who rules the house and who sets the guidelines when it came to us. Dad would've let us do things that probably would've landed the two of us in the emergency room more often than not.

"We had a deal," Dad says to Asher, still staring at him.

Asher sighs, pressing the off button on his new and extremely expensive phone before shoving it into the back pocket of his jeans. "Whatever," he mutters.

My mother rolls her eyes. "Boys are the worst, baby. The. Worst. If you're going to have kids, only have girls."

"I don't think it works that way, Mom," I tell her, pushing my cap back as it starts to slip. "This thing is pissing me off."

She looks around, trying to make heads or tails of the mess I've made in my apartment as I packed up the last four years of my life in the last week. "Do you have bobby pins? We can make it so that sucker doesn't move."

I nod and run to the bathroom, grabbing a few I'd found lying around when I was packing and left there just in case I'd need them. "Here," I tell her as I rush back to stand in front of her, my cap halfway down my forehead and the top covering my eyes. "Please help me."

Mom laughs, taking the bobby pins from my hands. "Girl, what would you do without me?"

"I can't imagine a world without you, Mom," I admit because, damn it, I can't.

She and I may fight. Hell, we are too much alike not to have some knock-down-drag-out arguments from time to time. But a world without Max Gallo isn't a world I ever want to live in.

Mom pushes my cap back, using her teeth to pry open the metal pins. "I'm not going anywhere, sweetheart. Don't look so sad," she tells me as she pushes the first pin into my hair, anchoring my cap.

"I know," I tell her, standing completely still so she doesn't shove one into my skull. "But everything's changing. I'm getting older, and by default, so are you."

"Child, you're twenty-two, and I'm forty."

"Mom."

"Fortyish?" She smiles.

"Close enough," I say, holding back my laughter.

"We have many years, and getting older doesn't have to be scary. Believe it or not, life gets better the older you get."

"It does?" I furrow my brows because I can remember some pretty damn great times in high school without a single care or worry in the world.

"You already found love. Soon, you'll get married and have kids."

"You're not proving your points," I say flatly.

She chuckles, opening another bobby pin with her teeth. "Marriage is the fun part, and kids…"

"Suck," I reply, letting my gaze drift to Asher.

"Stop that," she tells me, jamming the next bobby pin into my hair a little harder. "I love you and your brother. If I could've, I would've had way more kids."

I gasp. "That would've been awful. Really, really awful."

"Fuck that," Asher mumbles, earning him a slap on the back of the head from my father.

"Language," Dad warns him.

"That's some bullshit," Asher whispers, and right on cue, another hit, causing his head to pitch forward. "Okay. Okay." He lifts his hands, backing away far enough so that he's out of arm's reach of my dad. "I'll stop. I'll stop."

"Your daddy and I got started late in life or else we would've had a big family. There's nothing more wonderful than having a baby stare up at you like the sun and moon revolve around you. You'll know the joy someday."

"Not yet," I tell her, unable to keep the grimace off my face. "I'm in no rush."

Ma places the final bobby pin and gives the cap a good yank, but the sucker doesn't move. "There." She smiles and moves her hands back to my shoulders. "Don't rush into anything, baby. Life goes too fast, but…" she says, and with Maxine, there's always a but. "Don't wait too long either. Life doesn't always play by your rules."

"Ain't that the truth," I mutter.

"Where's Mammoth?" Dad asks, looking around my apartment like I'm hiding him somewhere.

"He and his mom are almost here," I tell him as he pokes his head into my bedroom. "They slept at our place last night and got on the road early."

My father blanches, still hating the idea that I'm moving in with Mammoth. He keeps calling it living in sin, which is laughable coming from him. "They should've stayed at the hotel like us."

"Motel," my mother corrects him. "There isn't a decent hotel near here for fifty miles. Why a big college town like this only has sleazy-ass motels is beyond me."

"They rent rooms by the hour," Asher announces, earning curious looks from my parents. "What? It was on the neon sign out front." He shrugs, collapsing onto the couch, making the old girl creak.

"No more talking," my dad tells him, pointing his finger at Asher.

Asher stretches his long arms across the top of the couch. "No phone. No talking. What am I supposed to do?"

"Just sit there and look pretty," I sass.

He smiles. "I can do that all day long, sis."

I roll my eyes this time. "You love yourself, don't you?"

He turns his head, kissing one of his biceps. "What's not to love?"

I gag. "Do the girls fall for your attitude?"

He nods, smirking. "The ladies love everything about me."

"Oh Lord," Mom mutters. "If we make it to his eighteenth birthday without becoming grandparents, I'll claim it as a victory." She finishes zipping up my gown, making me feel somehow claustrophobic even with the material voluminous enough I could make myself a human hot air balloon. "Between the two of you, I should have a full head of gray hair and tons of wrinkles."

"Ma, you have one wrinkle on your face."

She looks me dead in the eye, lifting an eyebrow,

head tilted. "Black don't crack, baby. Remember that. Lord knows you two tried to prove that saying wrong but failed."

I chuckle, and so does Asher. "You're ridiculous, Ma," he tells her, shaking his head. "You know that isn't true, and I have just as much white in me as black."

"You'll age better than most." She just levels Asher with her gaze, because he hasn't stopped laughing, motioning for him to get up. "Come here and show me a wrinkle on my face."

"Don't fall for the trap," Dad whispers. "If you want to keep breathing, do not move."

Mom tilts her head, lips twisted, waiting.

"You're the most beautiful woman in the world. You haven't aged a day," Asher says, his eyes moving from my mom to my dad, who's giving him a not so subtle thumbs-up.

"Smart boy," Dad mutters.

"Mm-hmm," Mom grumbles, turning back to face me. "Men are the worst."

"They are sometimes," I tell her, smiling as my brother gives me the middle finger. "But they have good points too."

"She's in love," Asher says, like somehow this is news.

"She's young," Dad replies to him with a shrug.

"She may be young, baby, but she found her man. There's no changing that. You're just going to have to deal with the simple fact that our baby is about to grow up, get married, and someday, give us a grandchild."

Just then, as if Jessica heard the word grandchild and willed herself to my location, she and Mammoth walk through the door of my apartment.

My eyes widen as I soak him in.

He's dressed more like a businessman than a biker. Hair pulled back. Clean and crisp white dress shirt with a few buttons undone at the top. Black slacks, which hug his thighs and crotch in just the right way to drive every grandmother, mother, and college girl crazy with lust.

Freaking great.

I'll be beating them off with a stick after the ceremony when it's time for pictures. I don't need a crystal ball to know that's in our future.

My mom turns and freezes, no doubt getting herself a giant dose of Mammoth. "Well, Jesus," she whispers. "The man sure does clean up nice."

"We're here," Jessica announces, clutching her handbag to her body and dressed in a flowery sundress like always.

Mammoth is staring at me as I gawk at him. The smile on his face is immediate. "Damn, princess. You look amazing."

I pull at the material again, showing him just how big the stupid thing is. "I look ridiculous."

He shakes his head, moving toward me with nothing but pure male energy and lust in his gray eyes. "I'm so fucking proud of you," he says, wrapping his arms around me, hugging me so tight I almost can't breathe. "My girl has a college degree."

"Not yet, sparky," I whisper, forcing the words out as he pushes all the air from my body. "But soon."

"We're going to have such great-looking grandbabies, aren't we, Maxine?" Jessica asks my mother, standing next to her and watching us.

He finally loosens his hold, still smiling and staring at me with so much love, I feel it deep in my soul. "They'll never give up, will they?"

"Nope. I don't think they will."

"Your grandma is the worst, though."

"Which one?" I laugh. "Because they're both insane."

"Should we?" he asks, looking innocent and serious.

My eyes widen. "Um. No. Are you kidding me?"

"Thank God." He smiles, gripping my sides. "I need some time to enjoy my woman being at my side before I'm willing to share her with a tiny human."

"Alone time sounds so perfect. I can't wait to officially move in to our house instead of just being a weekender."

Three months ago, we finally put down roots and purchased our first house together. I'd spent a few nights at the garage, hating every minute of it, and eventually put my foot down, telling him things needed to change before I graduated. We closed on the house and took possession a month later.

It is absolutely perfect. It is nothing big or fancy, but it has everything we need. Three bedrooms, two bathrooms, a small living room, a decent kitchen, and a backyard with a pool that will be where I spend most of my time when it isn't hot enough to boil an egg on the pavement.

"It's been lonely there without you," he says softly.

I press my hand against his chest, feeling the warmth and hardness of his body. "Well, you're about to have so much of me, you're going to get sick real quick."

"Impossible," he murmurs, nuzzling into my neck and pressing his lips to my skin. "I'll never get enough."

"You two going to make that baby in front of us all?" Asher asks, followed by a slap and an *ouch*.

"Shut up, child."

"I'm just saying, if I were mackin' on a girl like that in front of you…"

"You better keep that mack to yourself, young man," Mom tells him.

I laugh both from her words and the way Mammoth's beard tickles the skin near my ear.

"Let's go. The ceremony starts in less than two hours, and I want to get a good seat," Mom tells us, snapping her fingers.

Mammoth and I stare at each other, passing so many words without saying anything at all.

Our future is about to start.

CHAPTER
NINETEEN
MAMMOTH

"WOW," Tamara says, stepping into the backyard of our house, taking in the decorations. "You did this?"

I shake my head, motioning toward her cousins. "Gigi, Pike, Lily, and Jett did all this while we were gone."

Tamara covers her mouth, tears starting to form in her eyes. "This is so…" Rarely is she ever speechless, but in this moment, she is.

I slide my arm around her shoulders, pulling her close. "They did damn good, didn't they? The girls picked everything out, and the guys put it all up."

Lights and balloons are everywhere, hanging from tree to tree, crisscrossing the entire backyard. There are large round tables with beautiful wooden chairs scattered underneath the lights, enough for the entire family. It almost looks like a small wedding reception instead of a college graduation.

"It's absolutely perfect," she whispers, curling her arm around my back and holding me tight. "I just can't believe you went to all this trouble."

"Princess, you only graduate once."

"Well, technically, this is my second," she teases, squeezing me.

"First one with me, and college is a huge freaking deal."

Tam shrugs. "I guess it is. I never really thought about it. We all graduated high school and went off to college."

"My buddies didn't. We all joined the military. It may seem like everyone goes to college, but it's not true. But you did it. You achieved something that's still rare and impressive."

"Tam!" Gigi and Lily screech, finally seeing us standing on the patio, overlooking their handiwork.

"You're finally here." Gigi pulls her from my arms, hugging her. "We've been waiting forever."

"Do you like it?" Lily asks, rubbing her pregnant belly.

"I love it," Tamara tells them as she releases Gigi, glancing around the yard, soaking it all in again. "I can't believe you two did this for me."

"We had help," Gigi says, pitching her thumb over her shoulder toward Jett and Pike, who are busy near the grill. "Couldn't have done it without them."

"You four really outdid yourselves," I add, smiling at the three women I met not that long ago but feel like I've known my entire life. "You're amazing."

Gigi raises an eyebrow, tilting her head. "You're just now realizing this?"

"Will someone give me a little push?" Lily asks, wiggling the fingers of one hand and resting the other on top of her belly. "I have to pee, and if I move too slow, I won't make it in time."

I try to keep the horrified look off my face but fail. I know I fail because Tamara smacks my chest as Gigi gives Lily a gentle little push against her back.

"Come on, Weeble Wobble. Let's get you to the little girls' room."

"I remember when I was little," Lily whines, stalking toward the house. "Now, I look like I ate a watermelon."

"Eh, more like a beach ball," Gigi teases her.

"Shut up, asshole," Lily replies. "I can't stop to smack you because I'll never make it in time, but just know, I'm doing it in my head."

"I really feel the blow," Gigi says, glancing over her shoulder, rolling her eyes in our direction. "You pack quite a punch, babe."

I shake my head, laughing because I love those two as if they were my own crazy and sometimes annoying sisters. "You ready to celebrate?" I ask Tamara.

"Hell yeah." Tamara smiles. "Where's your ma?"

"She ran home. She'll be here soon."

"We're here. We're here," Tamara's grandmother says, walking through the house, carrying a tray of food almost as big as her.

I rush to her, grabbing it out of her hands. "You should've sent me to grab this. Don't carry such heavy things. That's what men are for, Mrs. G."

She peers up at me as she reaches for Tamara's arm to steady herself. "When are you going to call me Grandma or Nonna?" she asks me, smiling.

"Well, I…" And now I'm speechless and stupid. I've never called anyone Grandma. My mother's parents died before I was born, and my father's parents didn't like my mother, and before I was old enough to track them down, they died too.

"Say it with me," Mrs. Gallo says, speaking slowly. "Grand-ma." When I don't repeat her words, she reaches out with her free hand and gives me a light smack on the stomach. "Say it. Make this old woman's day."

"Oh Lord," Mr. Gallo mutters, coming out of the house a few seconds later, walking right into the middle of her request. "Baby, he doesn't…"

She turns to him, glaring.

He throws up his hands, glancing down. "None of my business. Got it."

I laugh, unable not to. Damn, I love them, and if I could've picked my grandparents, they'd be it. "Grandma," I whisper, the word sounding so foreign on my tongue.

Mrs. Gallo smiles so damn big, the corners of her lips almost touch her eyes. "Again."

"Grandma," I repeat, feeling like a little kid learning a new word.

Mrs. Gallo flattens her palm on my chest, looking so damn happy. "Nothing else but Grandma anymore. Got it?"

I nod. "Nothing else, ma'am."

I get a hard stare.

"Grandma," I correct myself quickly.

The woman is tiny with her head of gray hair and searing brown eyes, but I am not about to mess with her. It will take getting used to, and I already know I'll mess it up more than once, but I'll do my best and remind myself often she's *Grandma* and not Mrs. Gallo or, God forbid, ma'am.

"Now, your old grandma is parched and could use a drink. Mind getting me something?" she asks me, not her granddaughter.

"Water, or something else?" I ask

"Something stiff that packs a punch."

"Make that two," her husband adds. "We'd like a

moment with the new college grad if you don't mind."

I don't say another word as I head inside, leaving Tamara with her grandparents, finding half the kitchen counter set up as a self-service bar with every type of liquor one could ever want.

"Hey," Max says as she walks in the front door.

"Everyone's out back," I tell them, motioning toward the sliding glass doors with my head.

"Drinking already?" she asks, eyeing me with so much judgment.

"Making a drink for your in-laws," I reply as I grab two glasses and fill them with ice.

"Do you know what they like to drink?"

I shake my head.

"Ma will take vodka with a splash of tonic water and lime. Dad—" she pauses for a second as her eyes take in all the bottles "—just give the man a cold beer. He'll be happy."

"Thanks," I tell her, grabbing the vodka bottle and starting to pour.

"What do you want us to do?"

"Damn," Anthony mumbles. "Every freaking time. The Cubs just don't have it this year."

"The season's just started." Max rolls her eyes, shaking her head. "This family and the Cubs. Anthony, go outside and say hi to your parents and take Asher with you."

They don't even look up or reply before walking out the sliding glass doors to the backyard.

"You doing okay?" she asks me.

"Yes. Why wouldn't I be?" I ask her back as I fill the glass in front of me.

She leans a hip against the counter, handing me the tonic water. "There's something off."

"Nothing's off."

"Ma," Tamara says, walking into the kitchen and saving me from whatever Max was about to grill me about. "Come outside. You have to see the decorations."

"Okay, baby. I'm coming," she says, staring at me for one more second before pushing off and heading toward her daughter.

"Thank God," I mutter to myself under my breath and finish the drinks.

When I walk back outside, the yard is bursting at the seams, with most of the family having arrived in a short time and walking around the house instead of through.

I stand there for a moment, a drink in each hand, staring at everyone. Not that long ago, I didn't have much of a family besides the guys of the club, and our parties looked very different and clothing was usually optional. Now, I am surrounded by a group of people connected by blood or marriage, oozing with so much love, I can only consider myself one lucky son of a bitch.

"Honey." My mother's voice is soft.

I turn, still holding the drinks, seeing her standing behind me. "Hey, Ma."

"You okay?"

"I'm great. Just taking it all in," I tell her. "Sometimes I'm still shocked by how much my life has changed."

"I'll take those," Max says, plucking the beer and vodka drink from my hands. "Hey, Jess. Lookin' good in that dress, babe. Tits are top-notch."

Mom blushes, waving her hand. "Oh, stop."

"No, really. I don't know what you did, but they're like *pow*. Right in my face."

"Just tryin' something different," Ma tells her, winking. "Glad to know it's working."

"Ma," I groan, wanting to talk about anything in the world other than my mother's breasts.

"Oh, hush," Max says. "She's single and not getting any younger, Mammoth. Let the woman have some fun."

"It's fine, but I'd rather not talk about her breasts, or at least, not have you two talk about them in front of me."

Max rolls her eyes, whispering, "Pussy," before stalking off with the drinks and heading toward Anthony's parents to deliver the beverages.

"I really like her," Ma says, wrapping an arm around me. "I can respect a woman who speaks her mind."

"I must too because her daughter is a carbon copy of her, and I'm crazy about her."

Ma laughs. "Tamara's your perfect match. I see the way you look at her. I see the way your entire demeanor changes when she walks into the room. She's the one, honey."

"She is, Ma."

She reaches into her purse and fishes out a small box. "I ran home to get this for you." Ma holds out the box to me in the middle of her palm.

I glance down, staring at it. "What is it?"

"Open it." She pushes it toward me.

Peeling back the lid of the tiny box, I hold my breath. The sunlight shines off the ring inside, scattering in a million directions. "It's beautiful, Ma."

"It was your grandmother's. She left it to me to pass on to my firstborn son." She smiles, touching my hand as I hold the ring. "I know you're going to ask for her hand soon, and I felt it was right to give it to you now in case. There's no one else I'd rather have wear my mother's ring than Tamara."

I bend, kissing my mom on the cheek. "Thanks, Ma. You're the best. This means a lot to me."

"You made me a good mother, honey. If you were any other type of child, I might not have been as good as I was. Being single, trying to raise a little one while mourning your father wasn't easy or anything I ever thought I'd have to experience."

I'd already had my eye on a ring but hadn't purchased it yet. I had plans on going this week and picking it up, knowing I was going to put a ring on my girl's finger, making it official.

"I love you," I tell her, curling my fingers around the ring before anyone else can see it. "I can't thank you enough for trusting me with this."

"Honey—" she smiles up at me, touching my beard "—who else would I give it to? It's you and me, but hopefully soon, there's going to be a small army."

"Ma," I warn.

She pulls back and puts her hands up. "I won't pressure you, but this old lady isn't getting any younger. I'd love at least one grandbaby in the next five years."

"We can do that," I tell her, knowing five years is something Tamara would be down with. We've already talked about it and agreed now isn't the time, but soon we'll start putting babies in the mix, or at least, start trying to make babies.

The sound of Harleys rings through the backyard, vibrating off the house. "Who the hell?" I mumble, turning and seeing no one.

"Hey," Tamara says, walking toward me with a

mischievous smile. "Gigi and I may have invited a few people."

"Who?" I ask, scowling.

"Oh, you know." She grins, batting her dark eyelashes. "Eagle and Ginger."

"Is that all?"

"Possibly," she says, drawing the word out.

"Tamara."

"Okay," she groans. "I invited Morris and Tiny too."

I roll my eyes, growling.

My mom claps. "I just love Morris."

"You better walk that statement back," I say, jamming the ring into my pocket as the two women peer toward the side of the house, waiting for the guys to get here.

"Come on. It's been a long time since I've seen them, and I know Jessica would like to see them too. Am I right?" Tamara elbows my mom and laughs.

"The guys here?" Pike asks, clueless to the girls inviting them.

I nod. "Gigi and Tamara asked them to come."

Pike shrugs. "Can't stop them. You know how they are. You okay with that?"

"I have to be," I tell him.

"Oh, stop. They're sweet boys," Ma replies, smiling like a love-sick idiot.

"They're not boys, nor are they sweet, Ma."

She waves her hand at me. "They're sweet to me."

"I'm sure they are," Pike mumbles, covering his mouth with his hand.

Dear God. Between my mother and Tamara, I swear they're trying to put me in an early grave. I saw the guys a month ago when they showed up at the garage, checking up on me and wanting to discuss business.

For the most part, they've left me alone, knowing I'm not going to be doing anything to put my freedom in jeopardy. Since the day Tamara walked into my life, I knew I was walking out of the club. There was no future for either of us there, but I'd be damned if I'd end up in jail because of some bullshit.

Even though I am pissed about Morris and Tiny being here, I am happy to see Ginger and Eagle, my two closest friends from the club. I'd been very careful with Morris, making sure he didn't know where my mother lived, and I made damn sure she was never around the shop when I knew he was going to pop in for a quick chat.

"Sugar," Morris calls out, leading the pack into the backyard. "You're even prettier than I remembered."

"Fucker," I growl, getting a smack from the back of my mother's hand to my gut.

"Shut it," Ma says through gritted teeth while smiling at Morris.

Tamara laughs again, squeezing my hand as she plasters her body against me. "I think it's cute. Look how happy they are to see each other."

"It's not cute."

Ma wraps her arms around Morris, and he lifts her off the ground, twirling her in the air, causing her sundress to fly up. She tips her head back and giggles like a schoolgirl, looking extra small in his big, burly arms.

"Relax, sparky. They aren't going to fuck here in front of everyone."

My stomach rolls. "Princess, if he ever sticks his dick in my ma…"

"You'll what? Ground her?" Tamara teases, laughing harder.

"One of us isn't going to come out alive."

Tamara smacks my ass playfully. "You'll do no such thing. I talked to your mom. They're just friends. She isn't interested in him that way, but she does like when he flirts with her. She said it makes her feel beautiful. And as a woman, I can understand the need to feel pretty sometimes, especially when your life is a shitshow."

"Her life isn't a shitshow."

"Now, it's not, but it was, and he was kind to her during that time. Let them flirt. Morris and your mom will never be a thing. I promise you that." She motions toward them with her hand. "Just look at them. Two people have never been more opposite, but there's respect between them. So, just relax. This is my day and not yours."

She is right. This day isn't about me. It's about Tamara and celebrating her graduation. Whatever makes her happy, even my mother flirting with Morris, I'll have to find a way to be okay with it.

I won't ruin her day no matter how much it kills me on the inside to see my mother soaking up Morris's praises.

"Dude, I've missed your sorry ass," Eagle says, stalking toward me with his cut over a clean black T-shirt and a new pair of jeans. "Look at you, living like a king."

We forgo handshakes, giving each other a hug in the manliest way we can, followed by a hard backslap. "You could have this too if you'd come over here and work with me."

Eagle shakes his head, pulling back, finishing with a handshake. "This life isn't for me. I'm built for the open road and nothing but trouble, brother. You know this. If you need me from time to time for a special job, I'll be here. But other than that, I have to stay where I am. Where I'm meant to be."

"Hey, Eagle. You gonna share some of that lovin' with me?" Tamara asks from behind us.

Eagle laughs, pushing me to the side to get at her. "The big college grad. All that beauty and brains too.

Mammoth's lucky he found you first because I would've snagged you in a heartbeat, baby."

Tamara slaps his arm, laughing. "You're a liar. You couldn't handle all that's me, big guy. You know it, and I know it."

"You're a lot of attitude to deal with, but I'm sure we could've found a way to make it work," he tells her, staring down at her.

"New men alert," Tamara's aunt Fran announces, marching toward the patio after exiting the sliders from the house. "Let me get a good look at them."

"Watch her. She's handsy," I whisper to Eagle.

He laughs, but when Fran gets right up to him and reaches out, groping his pecs and then sliding her hands to his stomach, he shifts his eyes in my direction as I laugh.

"Told ya," I mouth.

"This is my Great-Aunt Fran. She's the best," Tamara tells Eagle. "Frannie, this is Eagle."

"I know a damn good nest he can roost in," she says, squinting and moving closer to him, trying to get a better look, and pretending like she's blind when she isn't.

"Nice to meet you, ma'am."

"Frannie," she corrects him. "It's nice to touch you, Eagle." She laughs, but she doesn't stop groping until Bear pokes his head out of the house and barks at her.

"Her husband." I tick my head toward Bear, who's watching her with his lips twisted.

"Well, fuck." Eagle grimaces.

"Pay no attention to him. When he gets jealous, that's when he gives it to me best."

Eagle almost chokes on his own spit, pounding on his chest with his fist. "What the…"

I wave him off and shake my head.

Tonight has the makings of being one hell of an epically fucked-up night.

"YOU'RE BEING RIDICULOUS AND, frankly, a little insane." I stare at Mammoth.

He fluffs the pillows on the guest bed. "I'm not sending her home tonight. It's way too dark for her to be driving."

The her is his mother. And she's driven on these roads for eight months and dark roads in general her entire life. This has nothing to do with her ability to drive, but the fact that she's sitting around the fire outside, chatting with Morris, touching him every so often.

I drop my shoulders and cross my arms, keeping my eyes pinned on him. "Do you believe your own bullshit?"

He glances up, nodding, and keeps fluffing. "It's not bullshit, and they're calling for rain."

I laugh, shaking my head. "Is she going to drown? I'm pretty sure the car will keep the rain off her."

"You didn't see the radar. Lots of red and you know what that means."

I roll my eyes. "That you're seriously losing your mind."

Mammoth straightens and pins me with his gray eyes. "I'm thinking clearer than I have in years, princess."

I walk toward him, wrapping my arms around his shoulders and tipping my head back. "I was really looking forward to a night alone." I waggle my eyebrows. "Know what I mean?"

He slides his hands to my ass. "We can be quiet."

"I don't want to be quiet. This is our house, and your mom has a perfectly nice place ten miles away. I really wanted to try out that new swing we bought."

His fingers tighten against my cheeks. "Princess."

"Come on, sparky." I kiss his neck, loving the softness of his skin and the coarseness of his stubble. "Imagine all the fun we could have. All the orgasms I could give you," I whisper into his neck.

His body shakes with laughter. "You mean the orgasms I'd give you."

"Same thing." I smile, kissing him more and using my teeth because I know it'll give him shivers. "Don't ruin our first night here."

"It's not our first night," he argues, but his voice cracks, and I know I'm getting to him.

"It's the first night I don't have to ever leave again." He stares down at me as I peer up. "Pretty please," I beg, giving him puppy-dog eyes and pressing my tits against his chest.

"Fuck," he growls, almost lifting me off the floor with the grip he has on my ass. "Fine. She can go home."

"I'm sure she'll be thrilled to hear you're going to allow her to go to her own house."

He pinches my ass cheek, and I jump, instantly laughing.

"Such a smartass."

I throw him a wink. "It's why you love me."

"It's one of the reasons why I love you." He bends and presses his lips to my neck now.

I close my eyes, soaking in the warmth of his mouth on my skin, tangling my fingers in his hair. "Think they'll notice if we don't go back out?"

He turns me, moving me back toward the bed until my legs bump against the mattress. My belly flutters, and my eyes dart toward the door.

"Don't worry. They're all busy, and no one knows where we are," he tells me, pushing me back onto the bed. He kneels quickly, reaching for my jean shorts. "Lift up."

I don't hesitate as I lift my ass from the mattress,

letting him pull my shorts down my legs. The material is barely away from my feet when his mouth is on me and I'm moaning out his name, tangling my fingers in the top of his hair. "Right there."

He hums his approval and slides his hands under my ass, giving him full access. I press my legs against his head, almost suffocating him, but locking him in place as my toes curl.

The man can eat pussy like he was put on this earth for that purpose alone.

He knows every spot on my body that drives me wild and brings me pleasure.

He can torture me, drawing out my orgasm for what sometimes feels like an eternity or have me panting in under a minute before the waves of pleasure crash over me, stealing my breath.

He isn't wasting his time now, with too many people outside and a party still in full swing. He doubles down, sucking harder, flicking that damn tongue faster, driving me closer to orgasm. I curl my fingers, clawing at the comforter and squeezing my eyes shut, gasping for air.

"Oh my God. Oh my God," I call out, pushing my pussy into his face as my legs start to shake.

Seconds later, he's pulling his face away, and I lie there like a giant puddle of happy goo. "That was…"

"Fuckin' fast," he says, wiping at his lips. "I

promise later I'll take my time and worship your body the way it deserves."

I blink up at the ceiling, still gasping for air. "It was perfect, but I'm not sure I can walk for a few minutes."

He collapses on his back next to me, leaving my bottom half bare. "I'm in no rush to get back."

"The party is really great. You didn't have to go to so much trouble."

His fingers tangle with mine. "I wanted the day to be special, and it wasn't any trouble. Even if it were, you're worth every second."

I turn my head, looking at him with a stupid grin on my face. "I don't know what I did to get so lucky to get you."

"It was that sass, princess."

"I thought it was my ass."

He laughs. "Definite bonus points were given for that ass."

I smack his chest before rolling to my side. "We should go out there."

"Yeah," he whispers, moving his face closer and kissing me gently.

"No Ma tonight, right?" I ask.

"No Ma," he repeats, but I can tell it's killing him to give in.

A few minutes later, we head back outside, finding the family just as we left them. The guys from the

Disciples are sitting at one table, but they aren't alone. Pike and Gigi have joined them and are deep in conversation as Gigi sits on Pike's lap with her arm draped over his shoulder.

As soon as Morris spots us, he gets up and heads our way. He fishes a white envelope out of his cut and holds it out to me as he gets closer. "The guys got together and wanted to give you a present."

I pluck the envelope from Morris's fingers and smile up at the big guy I didn't even know just a few short years ago. "Thank you, Morris. It's very sweet of you guys."

"Don't get too excited," he says, running his fingers through his hair. "We're shit at buying gifts. It's just cash."

"Y'all didn't have to get me anything at all. Just you guys being here means a lot." I step forward, wrapping my arms around his middle, and he tenses for a second, probably exchanging a heated gaze with Mammoth before hugging me back.

"We're going to take off in a bit. I just want to say goodbye to Jessica, and then we're heading back. Call if you two need anything, or else I'll see you—" he directs his gaze toward Mammoth, giving him a chin dip "—in a few weeks."

I twist my body, peering up at Mammoth with wider eyes. "A few weeks?" I mouth, but silently, because I know he isn't going to answer me until the guys have left, if even then.

"See you then." Mammoth holds out his hand to Morris, pretending to be civilized.

For a second, Morris stares at Mammoth before finally taking his hand and shaking. I breathe a sigh of relief because these two are intense, and Mammoth leaving the MC hasn't made things any less stressful.

They've rarely called him back to the compound, but when they do, Mammoth's in a shit mood for a few days afterward. Not because he hates being around the guys, but it puts his work at the shop behind schedule, and he has to work twice as hard to make up the lost time.

I wrap an arm around Mammoth as Morris stalks across the yard, making a beeline for Jessica.

"Relax," I remind him, resting my head against his chest. "He's leaving and without her."

As Mammoth grunts and watches Morris carefully, I let my gaze travel around the yard, taking in the kids and people who make up my big, crazy family.

Uncle Earl is holding court near the center, talking to both my grandmothers and has them both in hysterics in true Uncle Earl fashion. I'm not sure there's ever been a time when the man took much in life seriously, but I wouldn't have him any other way.

Aunt Clara walks over with Denzel holding her

arm. "We're so proud of you, baby," she says, smiling up at me with so much love.

"Thank you, Auntie." I reach out and wrap my arms around her, squeezing her softly so as not to hurt her. "It means a lot coming from you."

"Your uncle's proud too, but he's too busy keeping the women company." She twists her lips, glancing over her shoulder at Uncle Earl. "He'll never change."

"Men never do," Uncle Denzel tells her. "Brenda's tried for years."

"There's no changing someone like you," Aunt Clara tells him, tilting her head and shaking it.

"Like me?" Uncle Denzel touches his chest. "What's that mean?"

"Hardheaded and set in his ways," she replies.

He laughs. "You just described yourself."

I giggle, loving my family and their insanity.

"I need a drink, Denzel," she tells him, taking a step away from me as Lily and Gigi head my way.

"Okay, don't freak out," Lily says, holding her stomach and wobbling toward me with Gigi at her side, clutching her arm.

"What's wrong?" I ask, bracing myself for the worst news ever.

Nothing good ever happens after the words *Don't freak out*. I know this. They know this. Everybody knows this, and yet, they still say it, expecting people not to lose their shit.

Lily sucks in a large breath, leaning to one side. "I'm having contractions."

My eyes widen and my stomach flutters. "You're what? You're not due yet."

"The baby is coming," Gigi explains, moving her hand over Lily's stomach like I'm a freaking moron.

"Fuck," Mammoth mutters, looking around the crowd and homing in on Lily's other half. "Jett!"

Jett jogs over as Lily leans forward, doing her Lamaze breathing. "The baby?" he asks, touching Lily's back with one hand and her stomach with the other. "It's too early."

"I fucking know that. What else would it be? Do you want me to just hold it the fuck in?" Lily snaps, going back to breathing deeply and wincing.

Well, all right then. Lily isn't one to bite someone's head off and she doesn't often use profanity, but I'm guessing the human trying to pry its way out of her vagina is going to make us see an entirely new side of her.

Aunt Mia hears Lily's colorful language and glances over, seeing her daughter bent over in pain. Mia is on her feet, running toward us, but she doesn't look panicked in the slightest. "Okay, baby. How many contractions have you had?" Mia asks, kneeling in front of Lily so she can look her in the eyes.

"A few. They were light at first, Mom. I thought they were just cramps, but now…" Lily squeezes her eyes shut, holding her breath.

"Breathe, Lil. Holding it in won't make it better."

Lily snaps one eye open, glaring at her mother as she inhales.

"Let's get you to the hospital," Aunt Mia says and pushes herself up.

"Oh God," Uncle Mike says, always being a drama queen. "Is my baby having a baby? What do we do?"

Mia turns, leveling her husband with her gaze. "You're going to go to her house and grab her bag that they prepared for this and meet us at the hospital."

He nods, but there is nothing but sheer terror in his eyes. "I can do that."

"I'm sorry I ruined your party," Lily says as she stands straighter, holding on to Jett.

"Sweetie, you didn't ruin anything. We're having a baby," I announce, lifting my hands in the air, happy as fuck it's coming out of her body and not mine. "Go." I shoo Jett and her toward the front of the house. "We'll meet you there."

The entire family is in an uproar, starting to move around, probably all ready to head to the hospital too. I hope the waiting room is large, because there's no stopping the Gallos from attending the birth of the first grandchild of this generation.

"Should we send everyone else home?" Mammoth asks, rubbing the back of his neck.

"Let who wants to stay, stay. It's no big deal. You can stay here if you'd rather. I can go with Gigi and Pike."

"No way. I'm going. This is Lily, and I want to be with you," Mammoth says to me, touching my cheek so softly, my belly flutters.

"Rain check on the hot fucking, then?" I ask him.

He nods. "We have all the time in the world, princess."

Jessica walks toward us, holding a glass of wine. "You two going to the hospital?" she asks, glancing back and forth between us.

"Yeah." I nod.

"Give me the keys, and I'll stay here. I'll keep everyone company as long as they're here, and then I can lock up before I go."

"You can stay the night if you want," Mammoth offers.

She shakes her head. "That's sweet, Josiah, but I really love my place. I'll be fine. I know how to entertain."

"We're taking off," Morris says with Tiny, Eagle, and Ginger behind him.

Jessica's eyebrows rise. "Really? So soon? They

were just leaving, and I was hoping to have some company until the party thins out."

Morris looks over his shoulder at the other guys. "You okay to head back without me?"

Mammoth's entire body goes rigid.

"Relax, sparky," I whisper, grabbing on to his hand. "Nothing will happen."

"We'll meet you back there," Tiny tells Morris, slapping him on the shoulder. "Call if shit goes sideways."

"You can stay the night," Jessica offers, digging Morris's grave without even knowing it.

"That's mighty sweet, Jess, but I have some business to take care of early. I'll hang out a few more hours and then head back to the compound."

Mammoth's fingers curl around mine, almost painfully. "Better go the fuck back," he mutters under his breath, "if you want to keep breathing."

"Did you say something, honey?" Jessica asks her son.

"Nope," Mammoth says in a clipped tone.

"Now, go. Lily needs you guys. We'll be fine here."

Mammoth stares at Morris for a moment, and there're words not said aloud but clearly spoken between the two.

Touch my mother and die.

That is the gist as far as I can tell.

I yank on Mammoth's arm, dragging him toward

the house. "Get the house keys and give them to your mom, and I'll grab my car keys. Hurry. I don't want her having this baby without us."

"Princess, I think it can take like twenty freaking hours or something ridiculous before that kid's going to pop out of her."

I stop moving, a look of horror on my face. "That's some crazy shit. Can we just adopt?" I ask, and I'm dead serious. There's no way I'm going to allow myself to scream in agony as a baby squeezes its way through one of my most favorite parts of my body, giving no fucks about the damage or pain the little thing is causing me.

"We'll talk about it later," Mammoth says, taking the house key off his key chain. "Go get your keys, babe. Time's a wastin'."

I move, hauling ass upstairs to grab my purse and keys so we're not too far behind the rest of the family.

We've been waiting what feels like forever for Lily to have the baby, and the day is finally here. My graduation is nothing compared to a new life.

Things are changing, but this time, it is for the better.

———

"Breathe," Jett tells Lily as the doctor buries his face between Lily's legs.

Gigi and I look at each other, the horror clearly evident in both our eyes.

"Yeah, I think an episiotomy is needed."

Lily's been in labor for hours, and I'm exhausted being a bystander. I can't imagine how Lily's feeling.

"You're not cutting her," Aunt Mia tells the doctor.

"But—"

"No." Mia's voice is louder this time. "Lily and I talked about this a lot before tonight, and she doesn't want to be cut, and I have to agree with her. Only if it's absolutely necessary, and we're not at that point yet."

The doctor squares his shoulders, clearly annoyed by Mia's words and telling him how to do his job. "If that's what she wants."

"I want the fucking baby out of me!" Lily yells between breaths, legs open, holding Jett's hand.

I'm exhausted and running on adrenaline, swaying a little as I stand off to the side next to Jett and his mother, while Gigi is beside Mia. Uncle Mike refused to come into the room, stating he couldn't see his baby in pain. Mia told him it was best if he stayed out of earshot so he wouldn't get upset because, no doubt, there was going to be a lot of yelling.

Gigi motions for me to come stand next to her, but at first, I shake my head. I'm frozen to the spot, too scared to walk past the end of the bed, worried I'll catch a glimpse of Lily's lady parts all busted and bleeding.

"Come here," Gigi mouths, glaring at me.

"No," I mouth back.

"Yes." Her eyes narrow. "Hurry."

I throw back my head, careful not to make any noises that may set Lily off or cause worry from the others in the room. Slowly, I make my way down the bed, being extra careful to stare at the wall opposite Lily's spread legs as I make the turn. I breathe a sigh of relief when I've made the short journey without seeing something I'll never be able to unsee.

Gigi grabs my hand, squeezing. "This is awful," she whispers, leaning into my personal space.

"Worst shit ever," I grumble. "Who thinks this is beautiful?"

"Not fucking me."

"On the next contraction, I need you to push really hard, Lily. Give it everything you got," the older doctor says, moving his little stool closer and placing both hands between her legs.

Lily curls forward, grunting and pushing as her face turns red.

The doctor keeps yelling, "More! More!"

I close my eyes, the scene before me far too much. Lily's too sweet to be in this much pain. Now I know why Aunt Mia sent Mike far enough away. The amount of pain and noise coming out of Lily is too much for me to handle and most certainly would've sent him over the edge.

"I see a head," the doctor says. "The shoulders are next."

I cringe.

Shoulders.

Damn.

They're bigger than any baby's head. The thought of being split virtually in two and a small human magically and painfully coming out of my vagina makes me want to run to Aunt Mia's office after this and get my dumb ass an implant instead of the pill.

"You can do this," Jett tells Lily, kissing her forehead and trying to be so damn sweet. He's such a great guy and her perfect match. I never would've thought they'd work out the way they did, but sometimes the universe has a funny way of making things right.

"Shut up," she snaps at him between breathing and pushing.

"I love you." He smiles.

He only gets a glare in return.

Gigi squeezes my hand, grimacing as Lily starts to push again, her face turning all different shades of red and purple. "I'm going to pass out," Gigi whispers.

"This is worse than the video she made us watch," I tell Gigi before swallowing down the bile rising in my throat.

"A few more good pushes and we're there," the doc says, popping his face up from between her legs to give her a smile.

Lily curls forward, leaning against her belly like she's trying to push the baby out with her giant tits. Those seem to be the only great side effect of pregnancy. Her rack is off the charts, and she's always been the smallest-chested of all of us.

"The baby's coming," Mia announces after moving down near the doctor to watch. "Push, Lily, push."

I sway again, and so does Gigi.

We're not built for this.

We never should've been in the room, but Lily insisted. She said she needed our support, but so far, we've done nothing but stand here and watch in horror.

Less than a minute later, as Gigi and I clutch each other's hands, holding our breath, a tiny human appears from between Lily's legs, looking slippery as hell and covered in so much stuff.

"It's a girl," the doctor announces.

I let out a loud sigh of relief, earning myself a bump in the shoulder from Gigi. I turn my gaze from the bloody little bundle of joy in front of me to her. "What?" I ask.

"You were turning purple. I thought I was going to lose you for a minute."

"You almost did." I laugh, wiping at the sweat that has formed on my forehead. "So damn close."

"Dad, do you want to cut the cord?" the doctor asks, and I know it's my cue to get the hell out while I still can.

I remember the video. The cord and then the afterbirth. I witnessed my little cousin being born. I did what I was asked to do, and I'll always remember this moment.

The tension.

The pain.

The horror.

The freaking nightmare of childbirth.

"I'll be back," I tell Gigi, speaking softly because no one is paying any attention to us. It's all on Lily and the new baby, as it should be. "I'll go tell everyone."

She nods, and I walk out the door, wanting no one else in the world other than Mammoth.

CHAPTER
TWENTY-ONE

MAMMOTH

I LEAN BACK, the bottom of my boots propped against the wall, watching over the family. The men pace, mumbling at one another every once in a while, and the women sit in a tight huddle, talking about childbirth and everything baby.

Mia, Gigi, and Tamara have been inside the delivery room with Lily and Jett for hours now. Every so often, Gigi or Tamara would come out and update us on the progress, which felt painfully slow.

"Hey," Nick says, coming to stand next to me and mimicking my posture.

"Hey, man." I lift my chin, giving him my full attention.

"So." He jams his hands into his front pockets and rests his head against the wall. "I want to talk to you about something."

"Shoot."

"College isn't for me. I like working with my hands."

I've heard more than a few stories about Nick and his ability to pick locks, among other skills he's picked up from his father but never used for good.

"You going to work with your dad?" I ask him, figuring it's the only thing that makes sense.

Who doesn't want to follow in their father's footsteps, especially a dad as cool as Thomas?

He shakes his head, and his dark hair flops over his forehead. "We're too much alike and I'd like to maintain my relationship with him, so working together is a no go."

"I can respect that." I don't completely understand it, but I can respect his decision. If my father had lived longer, my life would've turned out very differently. Sure, I still would've joined the service, following in his footsteps, but I can't imagine I would've joined the Disciples afterward.

He turns his head, staring at me with his blue eyes. "I was wondering if you could use another hand at the garage?"

I blink, surprised he's asking me for a job. "You serious?"

He nods. "Completely."

I don't answer right away, too busy thinking of all the ways this could go terribly wrong.

"I promise I'll work hard. I can work for free for a while if you want to try me out."

"You know anything about cars?" I ask him.

"I know a fuckton, man. My dad and uncle have always been gearheads. Plus, I was the one who rebuilt my car over the last eight months since my ass was shipped back."

His ass wasn't shipped back. He was kicked out of boarding school for breaking the law, selling fake identification to his fellow classmates.

I rub the back of my neck and sigh. "I don't know, kid. I need everything to be on the up-and-up. The shop isn't a hobby. It's our livelihood."

He nods, shifting until only his shoulder is touching the wall and his back is to the rest of the family. "I know. I know. I swear I won't do anything to put your business in jeopardy. I need to start getting my shit together. If you don't want to, I can find another garage that will take me. I just thought I'd…"

"Yeah, kid. I'll take you," I tell him, knowing I can't let him work for someone else.

That's not how this family works, and Tamara will love having Nick around the shop all day instead of a bunch of guys she doesn't have any connection with.

He raises his eyebrows. "You mean it?"

"Of course." I turn toward him, standing eye-to-eye before I finish talking. "But if you do anything wrong or act like an asshole, I will feel no guilt booting your ass out of the shop and not giving you another chance. I don't run a pansy-ass place. First strike and you're out. Hear me?"

He smiles. "Loud and clear."

"You break any laws, and I'll beat the fuck out of you before I fire you."

He nods, still smiling like an idiot. "I'd expect nothing less."

"You start next Monday at seven."

He blinks a few times. "In the morning?"

"No. Most of our customers come after sundown."

"Really?"

I sigh. "No, you dumb fuck. Seven in the morning."

Nick laughs. "Figured you were messing with me."

"Can you handle it, or do you need your beauty rest?"

"Fuck off," he says to me, punching me in the shoulder.

I glance down to where his fist has connected with my body. "I hope you work harder than you hit."

He tilts his head, staring at me without any humor. "I can hold my own. Again, my dad and uncle taught me everything I know. I was going easy on you. I didn't want to hurt you, old man. It's the whole respect your elders shit and all."

I bark out a laugh. "Little fuck," I whisper. "I know I'm going to regret giving you this job."

He straightens, looking excited for the first time since we started talking. "I promise you won't. No one will work harder than me."

"Sure, kid. We'll see."

Tamara comes rushing down the hallway with her face pale and wide eyes. "The baby's here," she announces so loudly, I cringe.

The waiting room full of Gallos erupts into cheers and clapping.

"And?" Suzy asks. "Boy or girl?"

"It's a girl!"

"Fuck," Nick mutters. "Another chick."

I laugh at his stupidity. "If this family were all men, it would be horrible, and we'd eat nothing but hot dogs and burgers."

"True," he whispers, running his fingers through his hair, pushing it back on top of his head. "At least they make some damn good food."

"Sparky," Tamara says, walking up to me, still pale. "That was…" Her head falls forward into my chest.

I wrap my arms around her, holding her tight. "You okay? You don't look good, princess."

"I almost fainted," she murmurs against my shirt. "It was the most horrific thing I've ever seen."

I bite my lip, stopping myself from laughing harder and louder. "But now there's a baby."

She tips her face up, glaring at me. "Did you know a vagina can tear?"

"Um, yeah." I shrug, still holding her.

"Like riiiiiip," she says, emphasizing the last word. "No more pretty vagina, but lots of blood and then a human comes flying out."

"I'm sure it didn't fly."

She blinks quickly. "I swear to fuck, if the doctor weren't there, the little girl would've flown across the room like a rocket."

I tangle my fingers in her hair, pulling her face back into my chest. "Is Lily okay?"

"She's crying, but they're happy tears. If my vagina had just been obliterated like that, I wouldn't be smiling, no matter how cute the little thing is."

"See, Tam. The pain is totally worth it. Lily's proof."

Her head tips back again, but this time, her glare is harsher and deadly. "You're not the one who has to squeeze a human out of his body. It's so easy to say it's worth it when you never have to pay the price. So, don't give me a bunch of bullshit. I saw everything. Everything!"

"Then it's a good thing we're not having a baby for a really long time."

"A very, very, very, very, very long time," she corrects me. "If ever. I mean, we can adopt, right?"

"Anything you want," I lie, consoling her.

I want a baby that's a little piece of her and a little piece of me. A little girl or boy running around with long wavy hair, giggling. I won't push her, though, especially not after what she saw today.

She buries her face in my chest again, clutching the material near my armpits with her hands. "Thank you," she mutters into the cotton of my shirt. "Let me stand here for a minute. I need a moment to myself."

I stand still, letting her breathe, grounding herself even if it's only because she's attached to me.

Nick shrugs, pitching his thumb toward the rest of the family. I give him a quick nod before going back to Tamara and her moment of panic.

"One more minute," Tamara grumbles, twisting my shirt tighter in her hands. "Can we go home?"

"We can do anything you want, sweetheart."

"I want my bed and maybe a few shots of tequila so I can pass out and not think about what I just witnessed."

"I can make the tequila and your bed possible, but the dreams, I can't control," I tell her, smiling against her hair as I kiss the top of her head. "You want to stay for a little longer?"

"No," she says, pulling back and taking a deep breath. "Take me home."

"Want to say goodbye?"

"Just to my mom so she doesn't worry about me."

"I'll wait here," I tell her, dropping my arms and leaning back again against the wall.

As soon as she's gone, Pike comes up to me. "Well, now the pressure is on us. You know that, right?"

I nod. "I'm pretty sure you'll get pregnant before we do. Tamara's pretty shook up about what she just experienced."

Pike laughs, running his hand across his beard. "Gigi too. She texted me and said not happening anytime soon."

"But as soon as they get attached to the little girl, they'll get baby fever. It's inevitable," I tell him, shaking my head. "They may be traumatized now, but it won't last long."

"You need any extra help at the garage tomorrow? I have some free time, and I'm sure Gigi's not going to leave Lily's side for a few days."

"I could always use your help. I'm finishing up a rebuild on an old Indian."

Pike nods. "Text me when you're heading to the garage, and I'll meet you there."

"You got it, brother. I appreciate the extra hand." I turn my head, seeing Gigi walking slowly down the hallway, looking paler than Tamara did when she came out. "Your girl looks like Casper right now. You better go help her."

Pike's eyes follow my gaze, and he shakes his head. "It's going to be a long night."

"From your lips to God's ears," I reply.

"Ready?" Tamara asks, returning from speaking to her parents. "I need to get out of here."

I throw my arm around her shoulders, pulling her to my side. "Let's get you home and tucked into bed."

"And tequila. I need tequila."

"I can make that happen." I laugh and kiss her forehead as we start walking out of the waiting room.

The backyard isn't a total loss. A few cups and bottles are still on a couple tables, but for the most part, the guests cleaned up before they left.

I am pretty sure my mother had something to do with that. Her need for cleanliness and order probably overtook her exhaustion from such a late night.

"Sit," I tell Tamara, pushing her down into one of the chairs under the lights. "I'll grab the tequila."

"Don't bother with a glass," she tells me as she relaxes back into the chair and stares across the yard to the back of the house.

I take the keys from her hand, and she barely moves, too lost in thought, like she's still in shock from everything she saw at the hospital.

The inside of the house is cleaner than the

outside. I owe Mom something big for all her hard work and not leaving a giant mess for us to clean up tomorrow.

With the bottle of tequila and two glasses in my hands, ignoring what Tamara said, I go back outside and find her in the same spot. She is no longer staring across the yard, but upward toward the twinkling lights.

"The party really was beautiful," she says, tipping her face downward to smile at me. "You impressed me, sparky."

"I couldn't have done it without your cousins," I remind her, placing one glass in front of her and filling it with just enough tequila to be considered a shot.

"Stingy," she mumbles before lifting the glass to her lips. Her hazel eyes are pointed at me as she quickly downs the liquid and places the empty glass back on the table.

When she reaches for the bottle, I grab her hand and pull it in front of me. "Princess," I say, shoving my hand into my pocket to fish out the beautiful ring my mother gave me earlier. "I want to ask you something."

"Okay," she says softly and slowly. "Is something wrong?"

I smile, loving this girl so damn much. "Nothing is

wrong, love. Everything is actually right for the first time ever."

"Sorry tonight got turned upside down."

I kneel in front of her, grabbing one of her hands. "Tonight was absolutely perfect, and it's just one night out of many. We have the rest of our lives together to build more memories."

She tangles her fingers with mine. "Thank you for always being patient and sweet, Mammoth. I don't know what I'd do without you."

"You've given me way more than I have ever given you, Tamara. You walked into my life during a time I wasn't sure I'd ever find someone to spend the rest of my days with. There was so much darkness. So much anger around me. Then this dark-haired, hazel-eyed, fire-breathing, smartass girl walked into the compound, not giving two fucks about anyone or anything, and I knew in that moment, she was placed on this earth for me."

"Liar," she teases, staring at me with those hazel eyes. "It was my breasts that caught your attention. Admit it."

I run my thumb across her skin, squeezing her hand. "There hasn't been a day I've regretted meeting you or leaving the club. We're building a life together, a future."

She smiles. "We are," she says. "And I can't wait to start on our life together. Feels like we've been waiting forever for this day when I don't have to go back to school and we can start whatever crazy ride that is our future."

"I love you, princess."

"Love you too, sparky."

"There's no one else in the world I'd rather spend the rest of my life waking up next to than you. There's no one else who lights up my life and brings me so much damn happiness than you. I want a family. I want the babies—but not too soon," I add because now isn't the time to argue about her vagina and the *wreckage*, as she calls it, of the aftermath. "I want you to be mine forever. I want you to be Mrs. Josiah Saint." I lift up the ring, showing it to her. The lights from above hit the diamond, scattering over the patio. "Tamara Gallo, will you make me the luckiest man in the world and do me the honor of being my wife?"

She blinks, staring at me and then down at the diamond. Her eyes glisten, instantly filling with tears. "You want to get married?" she whispers, squeezing my hand back, but otherwise not moving.

"Yeah, princess. I want the world to know you're mine. I never thought I'd get married, but there's nothing more that I want in the world than to call you my wife."

She stares at me for another minute before launching herself against me, almost knocking me over. "Oh my God. Yes," she says, kissing my face repeatedly.

I laugh, wrapping my arms around her, still holding the ring in my hand. "You made me the happiest man in the world."

She pulls back, giving me her eyes. "You have to make it official," she says, wiggling her fingers between us.

I slide the ring on, and it's a perfect fit, thank fuck.

"Ask me again."

"Tamara Gallo, will you marry me?"

Tears stream down her cheeks, and she smiles as she says, "Yes."

EPILOGUE

ONE YEAR LATER

Mammoth

"MAY I HAVE A MOMENT?" Anthony says, standing only a few inches inside the room, holding the door open.

Pike nods and stands. "You got it, boss man."

"Good luck," Jett mutters over his shoulder as he follows Pike out of the room.

"Want me to stay?" Nick asks, not moving from my side.

"We'll be fine," I reassure him, motioning toward the doorway with my head. "Go with the guys."

Once the room is empty, Anthony closes the door and stares at me and I stare back. Neither of us says anything at first, and I wonder if I should've sent the guys out.

"Max is with Tamara," he says, running his fingers through his hair, with his other hand in the pocket of his tuxedo pants.

"Okay," I mumble, absolutely confused on exactly why he's here. Her father and I have always gotten along, but I've never felt like he's my biggest fan.

He steps forward and sighs. "This isn't easy for me to say, so I want you to let me say what I need to without interrupting me."

I wave my hand between us, staying quiet like he asked.

"When I met you, I did not like you. Didn't like you one bit."

This isn't news, nor is it a surprise. He wasn't rude, but I wasn't his first choice for his little girl. I'm pretty sure no one would've been good enough in his eyes, but I certainly didn't even make it one step up the ladder to worthiness.

"As I got to know you," he pauses, and I hold my breath, "I still didn't like you."

That's not exactly where I thought he was going with the conversation, but I don't say another word, because he probably still doesn't like me based off what he's just said.

"But—" he raises his index finger, tilting his head "—over the last year, I've watched you closely. I see the way you love my daughter. I see the way she loves you. Even when you don't think I'm paying attention, I'm paying attention."

And if he isn't, someone in the Gallo family is, and they're all reporting back, especially since none of them can keep a secret worth a damn.

"Tamara isn't easy, just like Max is no walk in the park either. It takes a certain type of man to handle them without overstepping. Being with a strong woman takes an even stronger man."

I nod, staying quiet, because the one thing I know about Anthony is once he gets talking, he doesn't stop. When I went to him, asking his permission to marry Tamara, it was a three-hour long conversation.

"I gave you my blessing when you asked for her hand in marriage because I knew you were the only man for my little girl." He moves closer, his eyes trained on me. "When I walk my baby down the aisle today, I'm trusting you to keep her safe and make her happy."

"I will."

He holds up his hand, silencing me. "I know you will. That's not why I'm here."

"Okay."

The hand again, but this time it's almost in my face when he keeps talking. "Today, as you marry my daughter, I want you to know you're not only marrying her, but you are also marrying us. Who am I?" he asks.

I raise my eyebrows, more confused than I was when he first walked in the door. "Anthony."

He shakes his head. "You're marrying into the family, and while your last name isn't Gallo, you're one of us now."

"Okay," I mumble, drawing out the word.

"I know you didn't have a father growing up. I can't imagine what that was like. I know you took care of your mother, always looking out for her and being the man of the house. But today, as you take my daughter's hand, I want you to know, you're not only gaining a wife, but I'm gaining a son."

My mouth opens and closes, and I blink, confusion gone and replaced by shock.

"I know I can't make up for all the years you grew up without a dad in your life, but I want you to know I'm here for you now and will always think of you as a son."

My nose tingles and I grunt, pushing back whatever sappy emotions are bubbling under the surface. "You sure about that?" I ask, thinking he's somehow fucking with me.

"Completely sure. It would be my honor if you called me Dad," he says, smiling a genuine smile.

"How about Old Man?" I tease.

His lips twist. "That'll take some time. I may be older than you, but I'm not too old to try to beat your ass."

I laugh, running my hand across my lips, trying to hide my amusement. "Pop?"

He nods. "Pop works for me. But—" he pauses and moves closer, placing his hand on my shoulder "—I want you to know you can come to me for anything. I will refer to you as my son in public and private. I will do everything in my power to keep you safe when needed, happy when you're sad, and give you solid advice when asked. I take my role as a father very seriously, but you can tell me to fuck off too."

I shake my head, placing my hand on his arm as he squeezes my shoulder. "No way, Pop. I've gone long enough without a dad, and I'm not turning you down when you're offering me something I've always wanted."

When I was younger, I dreamed of having a father. As the years ticked by, I knew it would be nothing more than a dream. My mother never allowed another man in, devoting herself to raising me, more than making herself happy.

If I could've picked a dad, he would've been like Anthony. He's chill…sometimes, but also strong, caring, and doesn't hesitate to show his love to his kids.

"Good, son," he says, making my eyes water as he smiles at me with pride.

"We're ready," Pike says, peeking in the door, his eyes moving between us. "You guys okay?"

"We're fine," I tell him, ticking my chin for him to leave us be, which he does. "Thank you for this."

A second later, Anthony's hugging me. "Thank you for making my little girl happy and becoming a part of our family today."

"Thank you for wanting me," I tell him, squeezing him tightly, never feeling more loved by another man than I do in this moment.

Tamara

I shake out my hands as the nervous energy gets the better of me. We've been planning this day for so long, I thought it would never get here. Gigi, Lily, my mother, Jessica, and the grandmas have been hard at work making sure every last detail has been taken care of. I'm not sure I could've pulled off anything this grand by myself—or at least, still been sane by the end of it.

"Relax," Mom says before licking her finger and adjusting my edges. "You're absolutely stunning. Mammoth is going to be speechless when he sees you."

"Were you nervous when you married Daddy?"

She laughs, nodding slowly. "I was a hot mess. I was a bundle of nerves the entire morning, but once I started down the aisle and saw him at the altar, everything else went away and nothing else mattered."

"It's good to know I'm not alone."

"Every bride is nervous. It's natural, sweetheart." Mom grabs my shoulders and takes a step back, drinking me in. "I'm proud of you and the woman you've grown into."

My nose tingles. "Mom, so help me God, if you make me cry…"

"We can't have that. No ruining your makeup."

The door opens, and Dad walks in, stopping as soon as he lays eyes on me. "It's official," he says with a sad smile. "You're all grown up and the most beautiful woman I've ever seen."

"Daddy," I whisper, choking back the tears that are still threatening to fall.

Dad runs his fingers through his salt-and-pepper hair, unable to take his eyes off me. "My precious baby girl," he says so sweetly, just like he used to when he'd kiss me goodnight every evening when he put me to bed.

"Do not make her cry," Mom warns him.

He nods, eyebrows raised. "We ready?" he asks, changing the subject. "Mammoth's at the altar, waiting for his bride."

My belly flips and my hands shake. "I'm ready." I

inhale deeply, closing my eyes, trying to clear my mind.

"Take your bouquet, sweetie," Mom says, placing the bundle of flowers in my hands.

I curl my fingers around the ribbon tied around the stems, holding together the most calla lilies I've ever seen in one place.

Dad reaches out his hand, waiting for me. "Let's do this before you get cold feet."

"I'm not getting cold feet, Dad. I love Mammoth. There's no one else I'd rather spend the rest of my life with than him."

"Good, baby girl. That's exactly how you should feel today. I'm proud of you, and I love you more than anyone, besides your mother," he says, glancing at her as she watches us.

"I'll meet you two out there," Mom says, giving me a small kiss on the cheek before leaving us alone.

I move toward my dad, careful not to trip over my dress and break my neck in my ridiculously high heels. "Are you doing okay?" I ask him because he's my dad and I know he had mixed feelings about Mammoth at first.

"I couldn't be better," he says, patting my hand as I place it in the crook of his arm. "I know how much Mammoth loves you, and he'll treat you the way you deserve to be treated. And if he doesn't..." his voice drifts off, and he pauses for a second "…he'll have to answer to me and your uncles."

I smile, holding back the laughter because, at this point, anything could make me cry. "He will. No one has ever treated me better."

"I love you, baby."

"Love you too, Daddy," I tell him, trying to memorize this moment for eternity. This is the last time I'll only be Anthony Gallo's daughter and not Josiah Saint's wife.

I've spent my entire life watching my father love my mother and being loved by him too. He taught me how a man should love his wife. He taught me about devotion, adoration, and never giving up.

We barely speak as we make our way through the small, dark hallway of the church to the closed doors outside the chapel.

Gigi is there, standing in front in her black dress, holding her bouquet of yellow and orange lilies. "You look great," she whispers, winking.

The music starts, and my dad fidgets with his bow tie. "I never liked these damn things," he grumbles, making me laugh.

When the music starts and the doors open, Gigi, my maid of honor, starts down the aisle, followed by Lily with Celeste holding on to her hand.

Celeste wobbles at her side, throwing rose petals from a basket Lily holds for her. She is so damn cute.

A perfect mix of Jett and Lily with all her hair, big eyes, and pale white skin. She eats up the attention of the guests, all smiling and laughing as she makes a spectacle of herself and her flower girl antics.

When they make it to the end of the aisle, the music changes, and I know it is our cue to start down the aisle.

"Last chance to run," my dad whispers.

"Dad," I warn before drawing another deep breath and taking my first step.

My gaze travels down the church to the altar. Mammoth stands stock-still, staring at me with the warmest and most loving smile. His chest pulls in as he soaks in the sight of me in my gown.

I can't look away from him, with his hair pulled back and the contrast of the tattoos on his neck against the crisp white dress shirt. The man can wear anything and look amazingly hot. It should be criminal, but in the end, he is mine and mine only.

Our eyes stay locked, and with every step I take, the nerves from earlier fall away. Nothing else matters except for the love we have for each other. I never feel safer than I do at his side. I never feel more loved than I do in his arms.

I've never believed in fate, but I know he was placed in this world to walk by my side for eternity.

No one else would have the strength to put up with me or the patience to deal with my shenanigans.

"You look beautiful," he whispers as I step onto the altar with my father's help.

"Who gives this woman to this man?" the priest asks.

"Her mother and I do," my father says, and I turn to him, holding back the tears that are again threatening to fall.

Dad smiles and releases my hand with a wink. He only pauses for a second and stares at me before moving back toward the pews and my mother's side.

Mammoth takes one of my hands as Gigi pulls the bouquet from my other. We stare at each other again, transfixed, as the priest starts talking and the guests sit.

I have no idea what the man is saying. I'm too busy staring at my future husband, seeing nothing but possibilities and love in his eyes.

The ceremony passes in a blur. Prayers, readings, and words of wisdom delivered from the man of God, and not a second of it will I ever remember. But I will forever have etched in my brain the way my husband stared at me during those passing seconds.

"Josiah, repeat after me," the priest says. "I, Josiah Saint, take you, Tamara Gallo, for my lawful wife."

My future husband nods and repeats the words, making my heart swoon. "I, Josiah Saint, take you, Tamara Gallo, for my lawful wife."

The priest continues, "To have and to hold from

this day forward, for better, for worse, for richer, for poorer, in sickness and in health, until death do us part. I will love and honor you all the days of my life."

Mammoth repeats the statement word for word, without even stumbling once. He squeezes my hands, staring at me with those stormy gray eyes that pulled me in from the very first moment.

"Tamara," the priest says, getting my attention, and I nod. "Repeat after me," the priest says. "I, Tamara Gallo, take you, Josiah Saint, for my lawful husband."

I take a deep breath, but this time, I'm unable to hold back the tears. "I, Tamara Gallo, take you, Josiah Saint, for my lawful husband."

The priest continues as he did before, and I repeat.

Mammoth reaches up, wiping away my happy tears with the pads of his fingers as I finish my vows. I close my eyes, letting the warmth of his skin dry my face. "I love you," I mouth.

"Love you too," he whispers back, ignoring the priest.

"The rings," the priest calls out, and Pike and Gigi step forward, handing off the rings to be blessed.

Mammoth doesn't let go of my hands as the priest says the prayer over the rings, doing the sign of the cross. "Josiah," he says, holding out the bible with the rings in the crease.

Mammoth takes my ring and holds it in front of my shaking hand.

"Repeat after me. In the name of the Father, the Son, and the Holy Spirit, take and wear this ring as a sign of my love and faithfulness."

Mammoth slides the ring onto my finger, staring straight in my eyes, and says the words perfectly.

"Tamara," the priest says, and I do the same, repeating the words, unable to take my eyes off my husband.

"I now pronounce you husband and wife. You may kiss your bride," the priest tells Mammoth.

A moment later, one of Mammoth's arms is around me, and the other is on my cheek, holding me steady. His lips crash down on mine, stealing my breath.

The catcalls from our friends are immediate, but I block them out because my *husband* is kissing me.

"Dear family and friends," the priest says, lifting his hands into the air, still holding the bible, "I'd like to introduce you to Mr. and Mrs. Josiah Saint."

Our friends and family filling the church cheer and clap, rising to their feet. We both turn, and for the first time, I allow myself to take in the guests.

There are so many people. More than I ever imagined, who have touched our lives in so many ways, making this day happen.

I don't know what I did to deserve this, but I am

the luckiest girl to ever walk the earth because I am blessed to have a man as good as Josiah Saint to call my own.

The Heatwave continues with **SPARK**! Nick Gallo may be the most swoon-worthy of them all! Nick can't turn his back to a woman in need, but he never expected the Hollywood princess to work her way under his skin and into his heart.

>> Tap here to read SPARK now

or visit menofinked.com/spark for more info and to grab your copy.

Download your free bonus chapters at menofinked.
com/mammoth

P.S. There's a Morris & Jessica chapter too.

ABOUT THE AUTHOR

I'm a full-time writer, time-waster extraordinaire, social media addict, coffee fiend, and ex-history teacher. *To learn more about my books, please visit menofinked.com.*

Want to stay up-to-date on the newest
Men of Inked release and more?
Join my newsletter at *menofinked.com/news*

Join over 10,000 readers on Facebook in Chelle Bliss Books private reader group and talk books and all things reading. Come be part of the family!

See the Gallo Family Tree

Where to Follow Me:

facebook.com/authorchellebliss1

instagram.com/authorchellebliss

bookbub.com/authors/chelle-bliss

goodreads.com/chellebliss

tiktok.com/@chelleblissauthor

amazon.com/author/chellebliss

pinterest.com/chellebliss10